HUNTERS FROM ANOTHER PLANET

The devils frowned and pointed at the cardinal's men, swiftly, one by one. A spattering of thin, white beams of light sliced through the air, and the cardinal's men slumped to the ground, their mouths open in surprise, their eyes boggling and dead. There was a chorus of gasps from the terrified crowd.

Scorpio recognized the Hunters' weapons, delicate daggers that spit out white-hot beams of light. They were secured, like decorative spikes, at the bearers' wrists; so it was that it appeared to the assembled crowd as if the guards were felled by a mere devil's gesture, collapsing with steaming holes in their foreheads.

Stunned and fearful, the crowd backed away.

The Hunters grasped Scorpio between them, leveling their weapons at his chest, and hissed, one into each ear: "Where is the *orb*?"

SCORPIO

ALEX McDONOUGH

A Byron Preiss Visual Publications, Inc. Book

ACE BOOKS, NEW YORK

This book is an Ace original edition, and has never been
previously published.

SCORPIO

An Ace Book/published by arrangement with
Byron Preiss Visual Publications, Inc.

PRINTING HISTORY
Ace edition/April 1990

ISBN: 0-441-75510-0

Ace Books are published by The Berkley Publishing Group,
200 Madison Avenue, New York, New York 10016.
The name ''Ace'' and the ''A'' logo are trademarks belonging to
Charter Communications, Inc.
PRINTED IN THE UNITED STATES OF AMERICA

10 9 8 7 6 5 4 3 2 1

SCORPIO

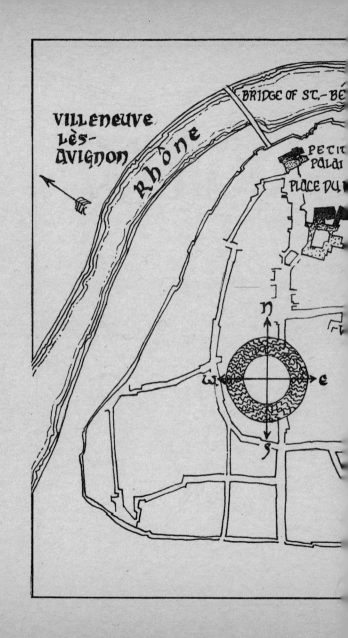

VILLENEUVE
LÈS-
AVIGNON

Rhône

BRIDGE OF ST.-BÉ

PETIT
PALAI

PLACE DU

N
W
E
S

IS

carnot

WISH
MARCER
EXTIER

◀◀◀ SYNAGOGUE

VIGNON

1351

Prologue
Scorpio Landing

Maybe they've killed me.
I think I'm not on Terrapin anymore.

The palace is gone, the ramparts and corridors of the Hunter stronghold, the steely cities and liquid globes of the vegetable gardens. I am seated in a strange field. The earth is unfamiliarly scented, cold and muddy, not spongy, not mossy. There is no dome. A single, pale moon. Grasses I've never seen, primitively sown in soil rather than water.
This is not Terrapin. So I have escaped.
Deity help me, perhaps I have died.

I remember the laserfire, I know I was hit. I felt the pain, it pierced my thigh. Where is the wound? *The orb.* Gracious Deity, I am healed! I can feel my body, it is whole. This earth, it is solid. It has a smell. I do not think that I am dead. No. But *I* have the orb—and I am triumphant!

I am triumphant, but where am I? I remember the noise before the swirling stopped, a loud, low-pitched whir; and the bubbling heat that threatened to burst my every molecule. And the pressure! as though blood and bone were straining to spring from the tips of my fingers, toes, scalp, pushing yet holding me still. Such a dizzying, frantic calm. Then the swirling and the watery greenness. Surely I was close to home?
I was certain I was safe, at home, when I let go of the orb.
The orb.

1

It must have been the orb. I grasped the orb, wrenched it from its pedestal with both hands, my mind squirting instructions: *Run! Flee!*

What a surprise—I did not run or flee. I triumph! Even the terror now seems sweet. Oho, I led those Hunter assassins a merry chase! A greased, wet skin will slip like a snake through a steel corridor! They were going to murder me anyway, so what did it matter? The threat of extinction made me rash! My people are never rash. We are a placid, thoughtful folk, the Aquay.

But the Hunters were always, and only, Hunters. Perhaps it's the truth, Leandro's little joke, that our Deity and theirs have never met. A bitter joke, to be sure. Still, we lived co-operatively enough until the balance shifted. How foolish we were, how blind. No one understood what had happened. But one by one, group by group, it seemed we were evaporating. The older ones just vanished, herded to the harvester camps, it was said. The younger ones, and the Speakers, we would find their leaking bodies flayed or sliced open, a hole from a Hunter laser burnt between their eyes. I remember.

We remained a thoughtful, placid folk. At first we sent emissaries to the Hunter stronghold, but they were never seen again. Our lives soon blurred into an endless night spent breathing through hidden tubes in underwater lairs, murky holes the Hunters would not penetrate with their instantly waterlogged skins. Mute, sightless havens. But we had to surface sometimes. . . .

How has this happened, what have I done?

It seems an eon ago that we began to hear rumors about the orbs. There was news of a new power source, discovered by Hunter miners on one of their forays to some fledgling planet. The power source, the orb, generated much excitement. Then it was said the Hunters had ventured farther afield, sought more, gathered another and another. The rumors stopped at three—three orbs.

Later, the few elders who escaped from the harvester camps said it was the orbs that changed everything. The orbs stimulated growth in the thin soil of Terrapin, so the Hunters no longer needed our hydrogardens. And the orbs had other powers as well. The rumors began again, of mysterious conferences held among Hunter elders, of strange bursts of light from within the stronghold at Chanamek, of the eyes of the Hunter leaders, glazed and far away.

I remember, it all began innocently enough. Our elders were asked to tend two experimental gardens, soil farms. These became the harvester camps where our old ones were forced to water the orb fields. After the first wave of protests, the disappearances increased. The murders began, public, personal, each calculated to foster terror and despair among those of us who remained. Witnessed. Our Speakers were exterminated methodically, ruthlessly, and then those who rose like a new tide to replace them. Leandro. And the young ones, why so many of us? We could not stop grieving, we were numb from grief. . . .

It was Leandro who told us of the Hunter system of assigning to each of their targets a personal assassin from their warrior ranks. They borrowed the custom from their own mythology, he said. Leandro was a student of Hunter lore. The executions were judged by their variety and finesse. Success was a matter of honor. "Scorpio," he told me, "speak to no one and swim alone. Take care not to imagine a future, or they will hunt you too."

Leandro was an organizer, not placid or numb. He planned to bore water tunnels into the two orb fields and free those who labored there. But he knew there was a Hunter assassin already charged with his particular death—a talented ore-finder, a fanatic diviner. Leandro had seen him. Or been allowed to see him. The Hunter had shown himself, another of their customs, a Hunter notion of fair play.

I didn't see him afterward. They told me how they found Leandro, whispered the unspeakable. Oh, they told me, but the horror lifted, and something inside me snapped. And then they were after me too, so I had no more time to think.

The solution seemed so simple. The Hunters had three orbs, we had none. I would bring my people an orb of power and try to restore the balance. I could not tunnel into the orb fields alone. But I could try to steal into the stronghold at Chanamek and capture the third orb. What could be simpler? They were going to murder me anyway.

My heart quickens, I see it. Could it have been just hours ago, just a day? I have peeled off my garments and coated my skin with the thickest of grease. My eyes are wide—with fear, I know, but I pretend I am one with my exophthalmos, reptilian ancestors and I slither on my belly from water hole to rivulet, slip through dried and dying aquagardens, swim into the sewer system of Chanamek.

I am in a pipeline, swimming against the current toward the city. Water spews past me, the overflow on its way to feed the now unused and shriveling hydrogardens. It gushes through my first obstacle, a sewer valve that opens and closes like a sucking mollusk, a dilating pupil, the mouth of a sea-worm in the great city wall. But I am enthusiastic, not yet dread-filled, and I push through as the valve closes. Something has happened to make me rash, and I dive into the gut of the raptorial Chanamek.

The sewer pipes are used to cool a maze of buildings and draw the moisture from the atmosphere so the Hunters don't drown. Hunters can tolerate very little moisture; their skins tighten on their bodies and they turn a fiery red. They rub themselves with sand to keep clean, and they take their liquids in their foods. The sewers are filled with chemicals and acrid Hunter piss. It has not yet been filtered and the stink of Hunter water sets off signals in my agitated brain: *Alert! Freeze! Dive!* My skin burns slightly, but the grease serves me well. I try to circumvent the messages of panic. I hum hymns of praise. I amuse myself with ironies. For once I am grateful that solid Hunter waste is deposited in clay pits, dried and pressed into bricks to fuel their filthy smelting furnaces. At regular intervals, I add my own piss to circulate beneath Chanamek. Ha!

The hours pass, the waters quicken. Like a stubborn sperm, I wriggle onward. Sometimes I am carried forth in a rush of water and am able to float for a time. Finally, in the distance, I hear the hollow roar of the cooling pumps, punctuated by metallic *plinks* from dripping chemical feeders. I have reached the underbelly of the Chanamek stronghold.

I prowl along the smooth steel wall until I find a wide metal spout attached to a porthole. It is sealed with gum to keep all traces of moisture inside the pipes. Braced on the spout, I push until the porthole springs open with a sucking *pop*! And then, *zip*! I'm through the hole, tumbling onto a pyramid of packets, chemical coolant stacked neatly below the spout. It, and I, spilling onto a cold metal floor.

The noise brings no one running. But I feel my first wave of dread. I am in a basement chamber. The air is so dry the salve begins to soak into my skin and I turn as gray as the steel walls. I must hurry.

The rest is a blur of corridors, pillars and fear. Like a greased shadow, I whisk through the stronghold. I am on the third level when the alarm goes off and I shimmy up a pillar and cling to the top like one of the grotesques on its capital. Hunter warriors thunder below me, helmeted, booted, dedicated, intense. No one looks up.

The word is passed along through the ranks. "It's a moisture seal break in Cellar 10." The squadron clomps around a corner and I continue my eellike progress.

The next alarm is a bad one. The Hunters have discovered they have an intruder. I curl around the top of the tallest column, one of a pair opposite a set of monumental burnished doors. I begin to sweat. Have they found my oily trail? But my luck is strong. The doors burst open and a Hunter baronet sweeps into the corridor, barking orders at a quartet of guards. "You two! Come with me to the cellar. I'll track this audacious Aquay myself! He's sure to set off a trail of alarms, even his stinking breath is wet! You others—join the honor guard in the orbarium!"

I try to breathe in short, shallow puffs to spread my humid exhalations thin. But I stare, horrified, as a tiny droplet of sweat beads at the top of the pillar and slowly, tortuously, dribbles downward. The baronet marches off toward the cellar and the two guards trot dutifully toward the orb.

I am following my Hunter guides, stealthily gliding, silently running like a crazed pool of quicksilver, when the alarms are triggered. One after another, closer and closer. The result is good—the guards increase their pace toward the orb. We approach a solid wall of icy steel, a seamless, mirrored barrier. I skate along the shiny floor, staying boldly behind the two guards so the only reflections they see are their own. My mind is gushing instructions: *Freeze! Play dead!* I override them all.

There is stomping behind me, and an enraged Hunter shriek.

"There! He is almost to the orbarium! Shoot before the doors open! *Now!*"

I begin to fishtail wildly, skidding toward a slowly parting wall of steel. Laser blasts like crossed swords, blinding lines of whitest light, are ricocheting from walls to ceiling to floor, weaving a web of deadly rays. I know I am moving like an unstoppable wave; but I feel like a river that is frozen in winter. I am the eye of a cyclone!

Around me there is chaos. Ahead of me, the surprised guards duck through the parting doors and take cover on either side. Behind me is a cat's cradle of deadly laserfire, blocking the baronet's party from the orbarium. The baronet is baying orders in a fit of fury. "Stop! Hold your fire! Don't shoot near the orb!"

The two guards flanking the entrance to the orbarium hold their fire as I whisk between them and streak along a polished floor. I am wounded, and my blood sets off alarms. I hear nothing but my own voice, and I am screaming. I see only a glowing shape on a single pedestal, it is miles away. I zoom toward it, I wrench the orb from its pedestal, is that another voice I hear? Is it mine? Leandro's? Saying *Scorpio! Don't let go. . . .*

The orb! I open my eyes. It is as I feared, I am still here. I find the orb. It is right next to me, as comfortable as a melon. Its amber glow has dimmed and it seems to want to burrow into the earth. Already it is nestling up to its center. The growth around it seems soft and lush, greener than the rest. Perhaps, like me, it wishes to hide, to delay the trek across this foreign field. But the next step must be taken. My breathing isn't labored, my skin is pale, there is enough moisture, it seems. The future must be faced.

I am in a fallow field, among dark brown mounds of earth. The mounds are covered with long, silvery grasses that are flattened by wind. There are two or three stone huts in the distance; they look like insect hives. There are trees, rooted in earth, not in water. A crag rises beyond the field. There is a stone building there too, very large, a stronghold perhaps, with towers, and slits in its walls in the shape of a cross. No Hunters in sight.

But I know I'm not on Terrapin anymore. Oh, my beloved Aquay. How do I help you now?

I remember my triumph! I've got the orb! It *must* have been the orb. And if the orb brought me here, it can bring me home as well.

Alert! Run! Flee!
Hush, my mind, there is someone coming. *Hide!*

It comes closer. It is speaking a language in a heated, scratchy voice. So a cognizant species, it would seem. Limbs like an Aquay, but with long darkish fur that springs from its head. Not armed, I don't think. Clothed in flapping garments. Female, by the look of her. But is she young or old? I cannot tell. Gathering greenery—a good sign. Perhaps we will have something in common. But that raucous voice! Oh, my ears!

Still, I have become no stranger to risks. I will stand and show myself! Perhaps she can help me.

Chapter
1

*T*wo hours after first light, Leah de Bernay had long since paid her five sous to pass through one of the three gates in the thick wall that separated the Jewish quarter from the rest of the citizenry of Avignon. A minute's walk from the gate, she had paused at the foot of the newly completed Papal Palace to gaze at the towers and ramparts, buttresses and arches soaring upward from their foundation of solid rock. The unyielding facades, twelve feet thick, were built of blocks of a gelid yellow limestone that had taken on an uncharacteristic, almost friendly hue in the pink light of dawn. But the glow soon faded to a cold morning gray, and Leah hurried on, down narrow and foul-smelling alleys to the turreted bridge of St.-Bénézet; across the quirky Rhône, the same shiny gray as the sky; past the aging tower of Philippe le Bel and the hills of Villeneuve-lès-Avignon, where the wealthy cardinals had their mansions; through outlying olive groves, heavy with autumn fruit; to a quiet forest that spread beyond the medieval city of Avignon.

It was a clear November morning in the year of Our Lord 1351. Leah loosened her cloak as the day began to warm, a small reprieve. Today the breeze was light and pleasant, but any time now the mistrals would begin to blow, freezing north winds that swept through the Rhône valley on their way to the sea. The mistrals were a mixed blessing, Leah thought. The unremitting, icy blasts would slice through the thickest clothing; but they also carried off with them some of the city's notorious stench.

For all its odors, Avignon in 1351 was one of the liveliest capitals of Europe, an international center of the arts that revolved around the learned and worldly Pope Clement VI. A generous patron, Clement attracted poets, architects and painters, scientists and scholars, as well as ecclesiastics seeking the lucrative benefices only the Pope could confer. The city was noisy, filthy, and overcrowded with fortune-seekers from all parts of the world: cardinals and bankers, emissaries and messengers, merchants and artisans, servants and soldiers, pickpockets and prostitutes, all ambitious satellites of the papal court.

The popes had been established, more or less comfortably, at Avignon since 1305. Clement had been Pontiff for almost a decade. And while Jean le Bon was newly King of France, Avignon belonged to the Holy See, recently purchased by Clement himself from the lovely teenage Queen, Joanna of Naples, Countess of Provence. The populace still vividly recalled Joanna's formal entry into the city three years earlier. She had come to face trial, accused of strangling her young husband, Prince Andrew of Hungary, and of having his body dragged by the genitals for some distance before having him hanged for good measure. The purchase of the city was arranged shortly before Joanna's absolution. Naturally, there was speculation that Clement had exchanged a regicide for real estate. But in 1348, the citizens of Avignon showed little concern for the affairs of state, there being a power far graver than king's or pope's to contend with; for in 1348 the Black Death reigned supreme. Its sovereignty endured for seven horrific months until, its hunger still raging, it departed for more northern haunts, having claimed fully half the city's inhabitants. By 1351, the half who remained were emphatically alive. They believed they had survived the end of the world.

The day was going to be glorious. Pausing at the edge of the forest, Leah sighed and stared at the sky, barely able to admire its luminous blue. She'd been feeling so restless and short-tempered lately. Normally, a day of freedom from the cramped Jewish quarter would have been a delight. But so far her outing had been spoiled by her own angry and confusing thoughts. Irritably she put a name to them: Aimeric de la Val d'Ouvèze.

Even his name had the easy grace of a young gallant. What a fool she felt now. How could she have known that he considered his nobility a given, and the code of chivalry just a game? Her budding knight had turned out to be a lout, and there was nothing to be done about it.

Leah banished Aimeric from her mind and concentrated on her herb-gathering expedition. Scouting the forest floor, she spotted an ivy-covered tree stump and yanked at a clump of ivy root. Good for treating her grandmother's failing eyesight, she thought. Maybe this will appease her. Grandmère Zarah wouldn't be pleased to learn that Leah had come so far alone. "Unmarried girls shouldn't venture forth unaccompanied," she would say. "I didn't go very far," Leah would answer. "You can drown just as easily close to the shore," Grandmère would counter. Or some such saying.

"Proverbs! Stories!" thought Leah, vigorously shaking the excess soil from the ivy root. She shoved the ivy into her apron and tucked the fabric into her belt. "I'm not a child!" she muttered, stamping her foot to repack the earth she had dislodged near the tree stump. Wasn't she her father's assistant? And wasn't he Nathan de Brenay, one of the most respected physicians in Avignon? Why, already she knew more than most boys her age; even her father said so. How could she be expected to learn if they kept her hidden behind the walls?

Today she'd been lucky. She and her father had planned to collect plants together. But just before sunup the doctor had been called to the home of M. Ferussol, the lute-master. His stomach was aching again. Leah had jumped at the chance to slip away by herself. Perhaps a good dose of solitude was all she needed, some room to breathe away from Grandmère's admonishments and Father's orders. He'd noticed her moodiness of late. If she wasn't careful, he'd have her drinking bitter draughts of wormwood to alleviate her melancholia.

Leah filled her apron with mosses and morels, ferns and barks, then headed for an open field adjoining the lands of the Benedictine Abbey of Montmajour. Father had said they needed more valerian for Mme. Roussillon's nerves—she *was* high-strung, Leah thought, but so charming! Did that mean they would be calling on her soon? It was at Mme. Roussillon's that she had first met Aimeric. How handsome and sophisticated he had looked, in his short tunic and elegantly pointed shoes! And how he had gazed at her! None of the boys in the quarter had ever looked at her so boldly. Much less dared to speak to her alone. It simply was not permitted.

So many rules! she thought wistfully. Often she had watched the carefree flirtations of the courtiers as they flocked to a banquet at the Papal Palace. Sometimes at night she could hear the music from the courtyard and banquet halls, wafting over the walls of the Jewish quarter. The ladies looked so gay in their finery. Perhaps some of them were immodest, as her father said. But how wonderful to laugh so freely! And to be able to talk with whomever one chose!

As her father's assistant, Leah knew she had had much broader experience of the world than the other girls her age. Not one of them had ever been outside the quarter after the gates were locked at night. That privilege was limited to doctors and midwives. Leah often accompanied her father when he was called to treat one of his many Christian patients, night or day. She'd been welcomed in Christian households.

Why did the Christians think they were so superior to Jews? Leah wondered. Their aches and pains were certainly the same—though the Christians bathed less, she had observed. But weren't they all respectful of her father's knowledge, and grateful for his treatment? They sought him eagerly enough when they were ill. So why were the Jews locked up at night?

"The gates are for our own protection," her father had once tried to convince her. Leah remembered only too well her nightmarish twelfth year: how her mother had gone to tend to a sick friend and died before she could return home; how the hideous piles of naked bodies had risen in the streets; and how the terrors of the Black Death were compounded by the attacks of an angry mob shouting that the Jews had poisoned the public wells. Pope Clement had issued a Bull protecting the Jews, and the violence in Avignon had stopped, though there had been massacres elsewhere. "They need a scapegoat," Grandmère Zarah had said. And every day she had told the story of the goat sent into the wilderness bearing the sins of the people, as though every day was a Day of Atonement.

But wasn't that all over now? Why didn't they take down

the walls? How ridiculous it all was, Leah thought bitterly.
Just because we have our own well water. Hadn't the Jews
died just as horribly as the Christians? Hadn't the pestilence
taken her own stepmother, and her newborn stepbrother, as
well?

Her father had been devastated. Physicians were as helpless
against the Black Death as were the astrologers, rabbis and
priests. Nathan had tried to console the living and see that the
dead were buried. But he had lost his only son. Leah knew
that her father had despaired of ever having another.

At the time of the pestilence, no young man wanted to be
apprenticed to a physician. But families tended to band together, and no one disapproved when Leah began to help her
father. For the past three years, she had worked by his side
daily, studying, trying to offer what comfort she could. She
had learned quickly, and she knew her father was pleased.
"She has a thirst for knowledge, just like a boy," Nathan
would insist. But she wasn't a boy. And lately it was beginning
to be obvious.

Grandmère was constantly bringing up marriage. Leah had
even spied her just outside the synagogue, talking to a go-
between from the nearby city of Carpentras. The sight made
her stomach twist with anxiety. What if they chose someone
she found repulsive? What if she had to leave Avignon?

Leah had been surprised by her own reaction. Ever since
she was a little girl she had looked forward to her wedding
day, had giggled with the other girls and daydreamed about
her bridegroom, the ceremony, a home of her own. But now
that she was old enough, she didn't want to be married! "Not
to any of the boys in the quarter, anyway," she thought. "They
are so serious and dull." *Not like Aimeric*. She squelched the
image. "Besides, I want to continue my studies. And I'm too
busy caring for Father, and for Grandmère as her sight dims."

Leah knew her value to the family was enormous, and Nathan
had seemed in no hurry to marry her off. Since her stepmother
died, she and Grandmère had shared most of the household
responsibilities. But of late, Leah had taken on more than her
share, as well as attending patients with her father and studying
when she could. Only last week, Nathan had suggested he find
a permanent apprentice so Leah could devote herself to her
"proper duties." At Leah's vehement protest, he had let the

matter drop. She decided he was just testing her commitment to her studies. But recently her father had been talking of marriage too.

It began after their last visit to Mme. Roussillon. Madame had introduced them to her visiting nephew, not yet twenty, but already welcome at court. Aimeric de la Val d'Ouvèze. Why, just last week, he had been falconing with his uncle— her brother, you know—Bishop So-and-So. . . . Mme. Roussillon had gone on and on.

Her father must have noticed how Aimeric stared at her, running his eyes from her face to her feet and then back again. His gaze was unnerving, persistent. She had blushed a deep crimson. Everywhere her eyes fell, there Aimeric would appear, boldly questioning.

"The arrogance!" Nathan had exploded after they left. Seeing Leah's confusion, his anger soon cooled. "You behaved very well," he told her. "You must cast your eyes downward when men look at you that way." He had gone on to make fun of the long, curling toes on Aimeric's shoes, twice the length of his feet. "How can he walk? And how can he breathe? His clothes are so tight he looks like a sausage!" Leah had nodded in agreement. But secretly she was thrilled. Aimeric was dressed in the height of fashion, and his taste was faultless.

Twice that week Aimeric had waited to catch a glimpse of her as she passed through the gate in the rue Jacob. Then it seemed she couldn't go to market without seeing him. Sometimes he would pass by her, very close, and whisper in her ear: "I yearn for you!" "I am dying!" "My dark angel!" "Your beauty is as a dream!" And soon she had been able to think of nothing but Aimeric de la Val d'Ouvèze.

Leah had heard all of the stories about Christian men seducing young Jewish women. But she didn't believe such a thing could be true of Aimeric. He waited for her every day. They had long discussions, or brief exchanges as time would permit. Once he had slipped her a book of the most current verse—not one of the dull moral tales that Mme. Roussillon was always reading. "This is what all of the ladies are reading at court," he told her. "It is the bible of courtly love." He quoted from it often: the *Roman de la Rose*. How impressed he had been at how well she could read! She had cherished the verses, and learned them by heart. Some days he would regale her with gossip from the palace—who had worn what to dinner, who had danced with whom, what music had been played. Always he told her what a bore it was to pretend to be gay when all he could think of was his "little Leah."

Their romance was impossible, and therefore pure, as only a courtly love could be. It was also a secret. On the days she was walking with her father, Aimeric wouldn't even meet her eyes. But she could feel his presence. He was so intense! So devoted! Hadn't he declared his love for her? Told her she was beautiful?

Hadn't he said that she could be a queen in a court of love? Their love had been ideal, just like in the *Roman de la Rose*.

Then, two days ago, he had asked her to sneak out of the quarter alone to meet him. Leah was alarmed. He must want to ask for her hand. She had spent a tormented day and a sleepless night worrying about how difficult it would all be. It would be lovely to live outside the quarter, to be able to come and go as she pleased. But her father would never allow her to marry outside the faith. She would have to convert. She could never do that; it would break her father's heart, and her grandmother's as well. Aimeric could lose his inheritance. It was all out of the question. Their love was doomed. She would have to meet him, and gently tell him that, for the sake of love, they must give one another up. Already she was pining for him. . . .

Then yesterday she had been out with her father and returned to the quarter through the gate in the rue des Marchands. Her father had stopped a short distance before the gate to speak to an associate when Leah spotted Aimeric with two of his friends, trailing lustfully after Rebekah de Milhaud and her mother on their way back from the market.

Her cheeks burned as she watched him stare pleadingly at Rebekah. She had seen the look before. Her heartsickness increased as she overheard Aimeric brag to his friends.

"Just think of them in there," he announced jovially. "Ripe fruits to be plucked!"

"Their beauty is exotic," agreed one of his friends. "But how can you even think of marrying a Jewess?"

"Who said anything about marriage?" said Aimeric. "I simply have a taste for something rare!"

The three had strutted away, laughing and jostling one another, without noticing the doctor and his daughter. Leah felt as though all of the air had been punched from her lungs. Somehow she had followed her father back into the quarter, stonily watched him pay their five sous and numbly gotten through the night.

Today, as she entered the fallow field of the Benedictine brothers, she resolved never to speak to Aimeric again. But what if he was just posturing in front of his friends? No, she had heard what she had heard. He'd been telling her lies. There was no sense hoping.

Leah headed for a bright patch of greenery in the meadow. "I must look for herbs," she told herself. Suddenly, all of her pain and humiliation came flooding back.

"Damn you, Aimeric de la Val d'Ouvèze!" she cried as her tears began to flow. "I wish a demon would sweep you off this earth!"

Cautiously, a naked demon rose from the field and spoke to her, hesitantly, in a warbly, watery voice.

"Can you help me, please?"

Chapter
2

At the sight of the demon, Leah felt as though all of the liquid had suddenly been sucked from her body. Her tears evaporated at once, leaving tight, crusty tracks that crackled along her cheeks, and her sobs dried into a knotted rag at the back of her throat. Her body grew stiff and drained of color, while her mind called up an image of Lot's wife turning to a pillar of salt. For although she was trying to run, her legs felt as heavy as sand, and they would not move.

This must be a delirium, Leah told herself. I was distressed, and now I am having a vision. She shut her eyes. She opened them. Then the terror began to rise.

"Don't be frightened," said the demon. The words echoed in Leah's mind like distant drips in an underground chasm. She registered little of their sense. But the liquid voice was strangely soothing. "I mean you no harm," it said. "I see we are both fond of plants. I gather vegetation in my own land, though it is all under water there."

Leah took in deep, calming breaths of air and willed her heart to slow down. She tried to think. There was a demon in the field. It did not disappear when she closed her eyes. It had stepped forth from a globe of glowing light and there it stood. It appeared to be real.

It had spoken to her. What had it said? What had *she* said? She remembered now, she had wished a demon on Aimeric, spoken aloud! She must have called it forth!

She gave a soft whimper of remorse and fear. Would it take

Aimeric away? Did she really have the power to make that happen? Despite her fear, Leah experienced a certain awed self-regard. Now that she had invoked this demon, was she also empowered to control it?

The demon blinked and stood quietly, expectantly, waiting for her to recover her senses.

She would have to try to remember everything Grandmère had told her of *shedim*. Leah had heard many tales about demons, *shedim*, both evil and benevolent. It was said they could assume human form. But she didn't know anyone who had actually seen one. That this one appeared to be real was fearful in itself, but although his face was misshappen, he didn't look malicious. A single bone swept sharply across his face, forming cheeks and nose in one unbroken line. Beneath this flesh-covered beak small nostrils showed, tiny punctures above a wide, lipless mouth. At the sides of his head were openings in awkward clumps of flesh, small and smooth as though the ears had been lopped off at birth and had long since healed. The effect, strikingly birdlike, was accentuated by large round, protruding eyes of a deep, soft green. These vanished completely when the demon blinked, leaving a seamless countenance with no lines visible from lashes or brows, which were absent. In fact, his body was entirely hairless—but quite human otherwise, with all of the requisite limbs in the usual positions and proportions. No wings that she could see; and a navel. But that would be only natural if the demon had assumed human form to come to her.

As a veteran of the plague years and a student of anatomy, Leah was little bothered by the demon's nakedness. But his coloration was another matter. He was as tall as she, and rather scrawny, Leah thought, with skin of the same pale, bilious green as some of her father's more miserable patients. This observation caused her panic to arise anew. What if the demon had come to afflict her with spleen?

"Oh, Lord, Creator of all things, grant me health and strength that I might resist all evil," she prayed aloud, fixing the demon with a defiant stare.

"Let it be so," Scorpio responded politely. "Sacred Deity, embrace your humble servants that we may receive your blessings."

● ● ●

Scorpio was pleased. The female being had welcomed him with a formal greeting or prayer. He sensed he had startled her, and observed that her eyes, which were outlined with hairs and separated by an angular bone, had widened in shock. Probably she was not familiar with his species. He stood passively still to allow her close scrutiny, and was glad of a chance to examine her in return.

Her form was female, there was no doubt. But she wore long garments that concealed most of her body: a close-fitting green gown or tunic, sleeveless, with contrasting red sleeves that showed beneath; a light-colored apron; a brown cloak.

Although she was eyeing him with unblinking intensity, she still seemed quite alarmed. Perhaps a response in kind would reassure her.

Scorpio fixed Leah with a reciprocal stare.

At the demon's unflinching gaze, Leah instinctively stepped backward, drawing her arms protectively across her chest. Then she recovered her nerve and glared back. She'd show this demon who was in charge.

Her expression turned to one of amazement as the demon studiously crossed his arms over his chest and took one step backward. Then he quietly returned her look. It certainly seemed he was taking his cues from her! Was he in her power? Perhaps he was awaiting her command.

"Begone, demon!" she tried, pointing skyward. At least her voice was firm, if not entirely authoritative. The demon dropped his arms and continued to look at her, sadly, Leah thought, or maybe with disappointment, it was difficult to tell.

"I'm afraid I can't do that," he said finally. "I apologize if I've frightened you."

There was that voice again, she thought, watery, pure, like the rippling echoes of the *mikvah,* the torchlit women's bath beneath the synagogue.

Leah's confusion mounted. The demon did not seem wicked. The sound of his voice made her feel safe. And the globe behind him gave off such a sunny light. He had said that he meant no harm. He had even condoned her prayer, and called for a blessing in return. Was he trying to trick her, to seduce her into passivity? Leah remembered stories that Grandmère had told of kindly demons who would come to the aid of those in special need. Maybe the demon intended to help her.

The silence was becoming unbearable, and Leah's curiosity was rapidly overcoming her fear, though her heart still pounded in her chest. She hoped it was not dangerous to speak directly to a demon.

"What are you, and why have you come?" she asked.

Scorpio relaxed a bit and answered truthfully:

"I am a being from another world, and I am not certain why I am here. My name is Scorpio."

Leah nodded, it was as she hoped. The demon had answered her call and would have to be informed as to her wishes.

"I am Leah de Bernay," she told him. "You, Scorpio, are here to do my bidding. I summoned you."

"You summoned me?" The demon's voice rose in a flutey trill. "And how was this done?"

"I cursed someone aloud in anger," Leah admitted, "but I may have been rash. I wouldn't want you to hurt anyone. You had best go back to wherever it is you come from."

"Rash, was it? I too know what it is to be rash—the results can be surprising, can they not?" The demon uttered a light warbling sound, not unlike a laugh. "But I have no wish to harm any of your kind, have no fear. I will gladly return to my world if you'll direct me."

"So you are a kindly demon!" said Leah, relieved. "But how shall I direct you? Can't you just appear and disappear at will?"

"I don't think so," answered Scorpio. "My people rarely travel, and I've never done this before."

"Well, try. All demons can appear and disappear at will."

"Perhaps I'm not a demon. I think not."

Leah felt her irritability returning. "What else could you be?" she demanded. "Did you not fly here from a world beyond?"

"I must have flown, in a way," answered Scorpio, looking skyward.

"Are you mortal? If you dry out, will you die?"

"Yes, I need moisture, that's certainly true," said Scorpio.

"You see? The only way a demon can die is to dry out. And can you foretell the future?"

"No," said Scorpio sadly. "That I cannot do. And I can die in many ways. Very many ways."

"What a poor kind of demon you are!" said Leah critically. Was it her imagination, or did the demon look crestfallen? His mouth, though lipless, had still turned downward, his lidless eyes had managed to droop. Immediately she felt remorse for her hasty words. Perhaps it was her own fault he was weak. It was her first time at invoking a demon, after all. "You must have some powers," she said charitably. "What is that ball of light at your feet?"

Scorpio was battling a wave of hopelessness. There were to be no easy solutions, it seemed. He was still stranded on an unknown planet. It was becoming clear to him that Leah hadn't summoned him, nor could she send him home. Obviously, she had mistaken him for some sort of supernatural being. What order of being was she, for that matter? Was she reliable? For all he could tell, he might be talking to a child. Nevertheless, he needed information. He must find the elders or leaders on this planet who could guide him homeward. He would risk revealing the orb to Leah.

With reverence and apprehension, Scorpio parted some of the verdant grasses that only partially screened the orb from the light of day. It had nestled into the dark earth, a marbled melon of a softly glowing bronze. Both Sorpio and Leah wondered at it for some moments. To Leah, it looked like the inflated bladder of some magical animal—metallic, but with the fine-lined texture of a skin. Scorpio, too, was studying the orb at leisure for the first time. Its peculiar rind or husk was unbroken, but from time to time he thought he could see something rolling or pulsing inside the small sphere. The effect was hypnotic.

At last he turned back to Leah. She was staring at the orb, her odd, fruity mouth wide open. "This orb has great but hidden powers," he told her. "I seek to unlock its secrets. Have you ever seen its like in your world?"

Leah wrenched her eyes from the golden light and regarded Scorpio with new respect. Perhaps she had underestimated his importance in the hierarchy of demons.

"I have never seen such a wondrous thing," she answered, "nor have I met with any demon before!" But even as she spoke, an image flitted through her mind. "Once, though," she added, "I did see a globe of gold, in a picture that hung

at the home of one of my father's patients, a Christian gentleman attached to the court.''

Leah paused, but the demon seemed unimpressed with her
father's connections. In fact, he was regarding her rather
blankly.

''In the painting,'' she continued, ''the Pope held a golden
orb with a cross on its top, cupped in the palm of his hand. It
was meant to signify divine power on this earth. But even an
orb of pure gold would seem dull when placed next to your
ball of light.''

''Where could I find the owner of this golden orb?'' asked
Scorpio.

''Only a great ruler, an emperor or the Pope, would own
such regalia,'' Leah answered patiently. Didn't this demon
know anything? ''If there is one here in Avignon, it would be
locked away in the Treasury at the Palace of the Popes.''

''I shall go to see this Pope,'' said Scorpio excitedly. ''He
is your king?''

Leah eyed Scorpio skeptically. ''Surely even a Jewish demon
has heard of Pope Clement VI! He is the ruler of kings, of all
Christendom. He may not be sovereign to the Jews, but we
live in Avignon at his mercy.'' Leah gestured in the direction
of the papal city. ''His power is far-reaching and unassailable.
Have you come to challenge the Pope?''

Leah's eyes sparkled with amusement at the thought. How
could a demon visit the Pope? And a Jewish demon at that!

''I wish only to ask his counsel regarding the orb,'' Scorpio
answered. ''This device will help me to return to my own
kind.''

''Why don't you use your wings?'' asked Leah practically.

''I have none.''

''Well, of course not, while you are in a human body. You'll
have to resume your true form!''

Suddenly Leah blanched. She remembered what Grandmère
had told her about demons, that they only regain their true
forms after mating with a human being. What if . . . and what
of that name, Scorpio? Didn't the sign of Scorpio rule the
reproductive organs? What was she doing anyway, standing in
a field, alone, talking to a naked demon who was trying to
seduce her with a glowing ball of light?

Leah's volition suddenly returned to her in force. With no

further word, she bolted from the field as fast as her legs could
carry her.

"Wait!" Scorpio called. "I have no other body! Please don't
go! I have so many questions, Leah! Won't you tell me where
I am?"

Leah did not slow down.

Scorpio felt a surge of desperation and homesickness as he
watched the panicked being flee. What could he have said to
have frightened her so? He followed her, calling reassurances,
as far as the edge of the field. But she only ran faster, and Scorpio was soon overcome by the exhaustion born of futility. He
stumbled toward the little stone huts at the field's edge. They
were simple cone-shaped structures, doorless, with earthen
floors. All three appeared to be deserted. Inside the first were a
wooden bench and some metal tools with handles. Gardener's
tools, thought Scorpio. These are gardener's huts.

Collapsing gratefully onto the bench, Scorpio looked from
the dim interior of the hut to the brightness of the field. The
greenery around the orb was a vivid patch among the grayness
of the sleeping field. He would have to move the orb to safety
before someone spotted the new growth from the bleak stone
stronghold on the hill. And he would have to find water soon.
His skin was beginning to flake, exposed to the atmosphere as
it was. But first he would rest for a moment, and collect his
thoughts.

Leah dashed into the cool silence of the forest beyond the
edge of the Benedictine field. The demon no longer called her
name, and she no longer felt his presence dogging her. Hugging
a tree for dear life, panting to catch her breath, Leah risked a
peek, past the stiff solid bark of the Aleppo pine, through the
sun-speckled shadows of the wood, to the field where her nightmare had begun. Was there a figure standing near the three
stone gardener's huts? She squeezed her eyes tightly shut, then
peeked again.

The field was empty. The craggy hill and blue sky, the
monastery, the gardener's huts and golden grasses, all stood
serenely in picturesque innocence, as if to say, "Who, me?
House a demon? Never!"

Leah regarded the scene for some moments. Her eyes stung,

and she wiped away the tears of relief that had sprung forth unbidden. There was no demon. But as her vision cleared, she could not help but notice a brilliant patch of green that seemed to have been dropped, like a silk kerchief, in the middle of the field. There must be an underground spring, she thought. How fortunate for the monks.

Scorpio's eyes wearily adjusted to the cool darkness of the gardener's hut. He had to blink repeatedly now, using the last of his precious moisture to keep them lubricated, and the flickering effect was irritating. But he was pleased to find, thrown over a primitive wooden wheelbarrow, a garment of rough woven cloth, once a light color, now a dirty white. It was a loose gown, patched at the knees, with long sleeves, a full hood and a belt of knotted cord. Good. His skin, now protected from the drying wind, would take on the light color of the cloth, close to the color of the female being. And the hood would hide his face. Perhaps it was his face she had found so alarming.

What if she had gone to alert others of her kind? Scorpio, dressed in the cowl of a Benedictine brother, set out across the field to collect the orb. It was time to find water, and to search for this Palace of the Popes.

He gently scooped up the orb and his dejection lifted as, briefly, his face was bathed in its amber light. His determination renewed, Scorpio concealed the orb in the sleeve of his robe, and set off in the direction of Avignon.

Cosily tucked away, the orb dimmed to a dark, burnished bronze.

By the time she neared the outskirts of the city, Leah had convinced herself she had had an elaborate hallucination, based on her anguish over Aimeric. But if she could face a demon, she decided, she could certainly confront a lowly mortal, and a lout at that. She would meet with Aimeric, and demand his apology.

Chapter
3

*T*he Rhône had darkened to the rich blue of tempered steel by the time Leah started back across the half-mile span of St.-Bénézet's Bridge. On the opposite shore, wan and regal, the Palace of the Popes rose from its throne of rock. Already the afternoon had peaked. Leah would have no time to watch reflections in the glassy river, nor could she slow her pace to study the assortment of travelers who streamed across the bridge in both directions. Today she would even forgo her customary game of counting, as she moved from pier to pier, the twenty-two stone arches that supported the famous Pont d'Avignon.

As the only bridge across the Rhône between Avignon and the sea, St.-Bénézet was a major thoroughfare. Merchants traveled to and from the seaports to the south, where they sent shiploads of Provençal goods, herbs and chestnuts and coral, to all parts of the world, and returned with exotic imports to delight the courtiers at Avignon: cinnamon, vanilla, perfumes. Tradesmen trundled cartloads of cloths and dyestuffs, leathers and wines out of the papal city to the great fair at Beaucaire, to sell or exchange for soaps and pottery, pipes and knives. Local traffic was heavy, for the bridge connected the papal city with Villeneuve-lès-Avignon, the cardinals' suburb on the western bank of the Rhône. Squires, clerks, nuncios and messengers attached to the Holy See crisscrossed St.-Bénézet daily, as numerous as mice in a night kitchen.

Normally Leah was entranced with the variety she observed on the bridge. It seemed as though the entire world found its

24

way to St.-Bénézet. Arabs and Africans, peddlers with donkey carts, prostitutes in their evening finery, adventurers fleeing their creditors, courting couples, escaped prisoners seeking sanctuary, lawyers sated from a day of bargaining, servants leaving the palace for the day, troubadours readying for the night's entertainment, knights and penitents, foreigners and foot soldiers—to Leah, in the clear light of late afternoon, all of the myriad faces and costumes of humankind looked equally safe and familiar; for she was haunted by her vision of the demon Scorpio.

She could not rid herself of the memory of his face, his changing demonic face: curious and avian, frightening and reptilian, strangely, undeniably human. She tried to rehearse the excuses she would make to her grandmother, but soon her mind would again replay her encounter in the field. She could see herself stamping her foot, freezing with terror, running into the forest. She could hear the demon's watery, wheedling voice, calling her name. And always, finally, her thoughts would return to the pulsing ball of light. Again she would recall its uncanny warmth, and again she would be suffused, just for a moment, with an overwhelming sense of the miraculous.

Leah turned her thoughts to the nature of miracles. The Torah contained many references to demons and angels and miraculous events. Were miracles always accompanied by angels? She had no doubt that angels existed, and as for miracles, why, the very cobblestones beneath her feet were evidence that miracles occurred. She knew the story of St.-Bénézet's Bridge by heart.

Since the time of the great Roman engineers, a bridge long enough to span this wide, wild stretch of the Rhône was thought to be an impossibility. Everyone agreed it could not be done. Nontheless, work on the Pont d'Avignon was undertaken in 1177 by the Frères Pontifes, a company of bridge-building monks who believed they were obeying a direct order from God. The heavenly message had been delivered to them by a twelve-year-old shepherd boy named Bénézet.

Bénézet heard the voice of the Lord call to him three times as he tended his flock, commanding him to build a bridge across the untamable Rhône. Though he was just a humble shepherd boy, Bénézet set out to inform the Bishop of Avignon. On his way, he met an angel who showed him the spot where the bridge must stand. Young Bénézet ferried across the river to relay the news to the bishop. But the bishop was annoyed. He disliked having his time wasted, and assumed the boy was mad. Bénézet became a laughingstock—until he was able to perform a miracle to prove his claim. The boy lifted a stone that was thirty feet long and seventeen feet wide, and carried it with ease, trailed by a stunned and rejoicing populace, to the river's edge, where he marked the very spot the angel had shown him. And there the impossible task was begun.

Well into its second century in 1351, the Bridge of St.-Bénézet was still considered a wonder of its day. The story of its divine inspiration was a staple among the Avignonese—particularly among a local group of thespian street urchins known as the "players of St.-Bénézet," budding young swindlers whose enterprise was tolerated, for a small consideration, by the keepers of the tollgates.

Leah, her mind on miracles, paused to watch one of the players ply his trade. The boy adopted an expression of the most angelic charm. His costume was artful: he had adopted the sheepskin vest of a rural shepherd, though it was likely he had never been farther from the city than the western end of St.-Bénézet. His mark, a gawking traveler, was unmistakable.

"Excuse me, sir," the boy began modestly, "but you appear to be new to our city. Allow me the honor, then, of acquainting you with the tale of the Miracle of St.-Bénézet Bridge!"

The visitor, ruddy and well fed, dressed in a new mantle and road-worn boots, was perhaps a burgher from a provincial town. His mouth had dropped and his eyes filled with delight at his first sight of the city with its imposing palace, just waiting for him beyond the bridge. Exhilarated by travel, interested and polite, he was pleased to listen to such a friendly youth.

"Sir, it is God's truth that this miracle was enacted by a shepherd boy no older than myself!" the player continued. Without missing a beat, he launched into a spirited and pious account of the miracle, complete with dramatic gestures and a small chorus of *oohs* and *aahs* from his confrères, who soon gathered with well-rehearsed spontaneity.

Leah had seen many newcomers to Avignon regaled in this fashion. Today on the bridge it was business as usual. The traveler was impressed with the hospitality and civic pride of the young Avignonese. The player finished his piece, and paused while the traveler complimented him. Then he extended an insinuating hand to collect his "gratuity."

The visitor noticed for the first time that he had been herded against a narrow cast-iron railing by a band of smirking urchins. Beneath him, placidly waiting, was the Rhône. Bewildered and hurt, he fumbled for his purse and withdrew a coin. It was a handsome purse of soft velvet, fastened to his belt by a flimsy cord.

Leah caught the swift glance that passed between the player and his partners. One of the smallest ran off immediately. Everyone knew that the players made most of their living by selling tips as to the size and location of a visitor's purse to the pickpockets who worked the tollgates, and to the "false beggars" who arrived for work at the bridge chapel each morning able-bodied and sighted, put in a full day of begging, blindfolded or strapped to a wooden leg, and nightly performed miracles of their own by regaining their eyesight or resprouting missing limbs.

Experienced travelers always had their tolls ready—four deniers for a wagonload, two for a horse and rider, one for a donkey, half for a man on foot and half that again for a pig—and strode purposefully past such entrapments with their purses well hidden.

Leah clutched her coins in her fist and hurried on her way. She felt a pang of sympathy for the newcomer. He was sure to have his purse cut before he was ten yards from the bridge. Previously she might have judged him naive and foolish, might have admired the wolfish art of the players. But today she suddenly grew angry, and all thoughts of demons and miracles flew from her head. She remembered instead a conversation she had had with Aimeric.

"The players are masters of allegory," Aimeric had pontificated. "Nothing could be more amusing than to observe their miracle play turn to a morality play. For beneath the surface of this holy city, at its very heart, do we not find corruption and greed? Do the players not provide a fitting baptism for outsiders entering the papal city, then? Indeed, do they not provide a service to these unwary newcomers—relieving them of their illusions as well as their purses?"

Allegorical the players may be, but did that make them admirable? At the time, Leah had found Aimeric's insights brilliant and poetic, and she had adopted his reasoning as her own, for she had wanted nothing more than to share in the views of the sophisticated Avignonese courtier. But were they sophisticated? Or was jaded perhaps a better word? How foolish and naive she herself must have appeared to Aimeric and his friends. Did they see her, too, as a tidy allegory?

Here she was thinking of Aimeric again. Her vision of the demon must have shaken something loose in her! For today she did not enjoy her role as a knowledgeable insider; rather, she found herself seeing Avignon through the eyes of a visitor from another place. Today a newcomer's unguarded delight at his first sight of St.-Bénézet's Bridge had moved her; and she was sickened by the casual ease with which a far from innocent urchin had exploited this moment of joy, and ruined it. Today she felt oddly impelled to act, as though she was driven by a secret strength, a warm ball of light.

Leah tarried until she was walking apace with the traveler. She would have to take care that none of the players noticed her—noninterference was an unwritten law on St.-Bénézet's Bridge. An opportunity presented itself soon enough. She was jostled by an overburdened coal porter, who in turn had stepped aside to avoid a fat cardinal, red-robed with a furred cloak, who rode a prancing steed home to his mansion in Villeneuve.

"Hide your purse well, sir," Leah mumbled, bumping against the beleaguered newcomer. "There are pickpockets about. And don't give alms to the beggars at the chapel—they are false." And with that, she hastened on her way to the tollgate, filled with a happy sense of accomplishment, and inspired to set the world to rights.

In the waning light of late afternoon, Leah headed for the Papal Palace to look for Aimeric de la Val d'Ouvèze. If he could not be found in the palace courtyard, he would undoubtedly be at his favorite post just outside the quarter, skulking near the gate in the rue Jacob.

Fresh from the countryside, Leah approached the palace with another of her senses grown as acute as a newcomer's. The eyes report beauty, she thought, but the nose tells quite another story. Even the elegant courtiers who climbed the stone staircase to the great arched portal held pomanders to their nostrils or scented silks to their mouths.

Leah watched a group of three merry ladies making their way to whatever banquet or entertainment was planned for the evening. Up the steps they fluttered like a trio of rare birds, multicolored, their fur-trimmed sleeves drooping almost to the ground, their headdresses decorated with feathers and pearls. Their laughter was cultivated, their gowns refined and their bosoms fashionably bared. How they could glide in their soft satin shoes, so self-assured! Leah imagined them seated at table, listening to poetic lyrics, perhaps, or enjoying sparkling conversation; drinking fine wines from crystal goblets, their long fingers plucking flirtatiously at grapes or spicy morsels. They would discuss the affairs of the world. Each guest would be served on his or her own golden plate. . . . Leah's confidence faltered as she sighed enviously. She suddenly felt very tired and drab. Perhaps she had best just go home.

Aimeric was stationed outside the quarter, casually scanning the street. It was almost sundown, and the gates to the quarter would be closing soon. Leah saw him first and withdrew into the shadow of a side alley, her heart pounding and her resolve melting. Why must he be there? How could she face him in her dusty clothes, with her headdress of twigs and her brooches of tiny sticks and leaves, with jewellike clumps of ivy root poking through her mud-stained apron?

Aimeric was dressed for a night at court, his wavy golden locks lightly brushing an ermine collar, his long legs encased in hose of sapphire blue, his hips just covered by a short, tight-fitting doublet of sky-blue brocade shot with shimmering silver threads. Leah watched him from her hiding place; he looked more gallant than ever. Bowing nobly, he spoke to a passerby, a stout woman who giggled and wagged an admonishing finger as she bustled home to her bread and soup. Leah felt an unexpected and uncontrollable surge of jealous anger. Was it all just a game to him? Would he flirt with anyone in a skirt? Pouncing from the shadows, she steeled herself to tell him goodbye once and for all.

When Aimeric saw her, his face lit up.

"My sweet Leah!" he cried joyfully. "You have come to meet me, after all! I feared I was never to see you again, and here you are at last. My love, why have you kept yourself from me? Do you not know that I wilt, I perish?'' Aimeric grinned and clutched at his chest as though his heart would burst through his sumptuous doublet.

Leah faced her suitor, her eyes flashing. "I am not a ripe fruit to be plucked," she stated vehemently. Aimeric stared at her as though she had gone mad.

"A ripe fruit?" He frowned, confused by her tone. Then quickly his face relaxed, and he grinned again. "Ah, it is a riddle. You are jesting with me!"

"I heard you yesterday in the rue des Marchands, bragging to your friends," Leah continued, wishing she had the nerve to slap his face. Her eyes were starting to sting, but her voice did not waver. "You have toyed with me unkindly. I have no intention of being sampled, then cast aside."

Aimeric's expression grew gentle. Surely this young girl had not taken his overtures seriously!

"I have no memory of any such words," he said, laughing lightly. "But if you overheard me with my fellows, why, you heard but strategies in the game of love. Mere thrusts and parries, challenges that pass between rivals. Meaningless trifles!"

Leah's eyes narrowed in speechless fury. Would he not answer her accusation, then? Did he think her so stupid? Her anguish was growing. But coupled with the pain was a hint of scorn, a scorn tinged with pity for the shallowness of this too-handsome man.

Aimeric, unused to coldness from women, was fumbling for words. What had she said about fruits? He mustered his charm and quoted from the *Roman de la Rose*. "To pluck the fruits of love in youth is each wise woman's rule, forsooth . . ." he tried. The raven-haired Jewess was staring at him with undisguised rage. He laughed nervously. Women were such moody creatures. Why, she was acting just like a woman of the court!

"Surely you don't think I flatter you falsely?" Aimeric whined coyly. "Do you reject me now as a ploy to drive me mad? Indeed, you have become a queen in the court of love!"

Leah had heard that one already; desiring to hear no more, she turned and fled into the security of the quarter.

"Wait, come back, my beauty, my only love. . . ." Aimeric's enticements followed her through the gate and into a narrow, twisting alley. Once out of earshot, Leah leaned against a gloomy doorway and let her tears flow into her sleeve. How guileful her elegant courtier turned out to be; how easily he lied! Only his riches separated him from the lowliest player on St.-Bénézet's Bridge, she thought bitterly. And the urchins must earn money for bread. But Aimeric—Aimeric seduces for sport.

Beyond the gate to the quarter, Aimeric shrugged. There was no understanding womankind and their whims—and it seemed the enchanting Jewess was like all others of her gender, at least in this respect. But was it not that blend of the familiar and the exotic he found so intoxicating? She was as mysterious as the most practiced of courtesans! How could a girl with her medical knowledge of the bodies of men be so naive in matters of love?

Aimeric shook his head. He would miss his little Leah. He was aroused by her unkempt beauty and amused by her thirst for learning; not least, he was flattered by her obvious admiration for him. But he truly had wounded her, it appeared, and this he regretted, for he had cherished a vague hope of bedding her. Perhaps another day . . . but tonight he would wait no longer. There was to be a feast at the palace!

Leah indulged herself in a last muffled round of sobs. If she didn't hurry, she was sure to be seen. In the Jewish quarter, everyone knew the business of everyone else. There may have been more space since the Black Death had carried away so many of their number; still the quarter was crowded and intimate. Her tears subsiding, Leah walked along winding cobbled alleys hemmed in by stone houses with red-tiled roofs. At least the stench was not as terrible as in the rest of the town. Here, the privies were emptied frequently; carters kept the open street sewers from overflowing; and the people often bathed. Leah dried her eyes and emerged in a small square near the temple, the well and the baths. She called a greeting to the butcher's wife and nodded to M. Emmanuel, the cloth-dyer, who waved back with purple-stained fingers. She would be home in time to help Grandmère prepare the evening meal.

The two-story house that Leah shared with her father and grandmother was larger than most of the others in the quarter.

The rabbi's house was by necessity the largest, as he was obliged to entertain numbers of visiting scholars. But the de Bernays had four rooms altogether, not counting the cellar. Upstairs, a low-ceilinged loft had been divided in two. On one side, Leah shared a bed with her grandmother, while her father, so often called away in the night, slept alone on the other, a very great luxury even in the wealthiest of families. On the ground floor the doctor had his study, and the family had their common room and kitchen.

Leah crossed the patch of kitchen garden at the back of the house, pushed open the heavy wooden door, ducked her head beneath the low stone lintel and entered the toasty kitchen. Already a broth was simmering on the hearth, fragrant with rosemary and onions. Grandmère Zarah was seated on a bench at a long wooden table, her back to the firelight, deftly plucking a partridge in the near-darkness.

"I'm back, Grandmère," said Leah softly, reaching above the table to light the oil lamp. "I've brought ivy root for your eyes." Watching her grandmother work so patiently, Leah regretted that she hadn't returned sooner. She knew she was spending much of her time with her father and his patients, just when Grandmère most needed her help. But the more she learned of medicine, it seemed, the more there was to know. Must she choose between Grandmère and her studies?

Once, the de Bernays had kept a serving girl to help with the household chores. But she, like so many others, had met with the Black Death, and the family had learned to manage alone. It was time that Leah speak to her father about hiring a new servant. Then she could devote her energies completely to medicine and become a renowned female physician. She would be respected worldwide. Welcomed at court. That would show the Aimerics of the world!

Leah passed through the kitchen to her father's workroom. It was her favorite room in the house, carpeted, with a little leaded window and a door that opened to the street. There her father's patients came to call, bearing their flasks of urine like the most treasured of perfumes, nestled in padded wicker baskets.

Leah unknotted her soiled apron and arranged the crumpled roots and sprigs of herbs in a wooden tray that had been specially made to fit in the top of a large ebony chest. Beneath

the tray, wrapped in paper or linen cloth, stored in beakers or
metal boxes, were the powders and balms, preparations and
ingredients her father prescribed for his ailing patients. The
pharmacy chest had been a gift to Nathan from an Arab physician with whom he had studied at university, and it was carved
with exotic designs that Leah loved to trace. Later, she would
return to sort her findings, separate the roots, leaves and seeds,
crush and dry them, grind and pound them, boil and strain
them, as required by the recipes in her father's cherished books.
But now she went directly to the kitchen to help her grandmother. There was a pile of turnips to be peeled.

"There's no hurry, child," Grandmère Zarah said as Leah
slid into her place at the oaken table. "Your father has been
called to the palace—an emergency, said the young page. One
of the cardinals was suddenly taken ill, and the court physician
is indisposed as well."

"He's gone to court?" Leah wailed. She wished she could
pound her fists on the table. If only she had come home sooner!
Perhaps she could have gone with her father and had a glimpse
of the banquet. She thought miserably of the reason for her
delay: Aimeric de la Val d'Ouvèze. Damn him, after all! Leah
choked back her anger and searched the shadowy room in
sudden panic. She really must gain control of herself, lest she
call forth the demon again. There was no sense blaming Aimeric for this anyway, she thought. Her father would never have
taken her on a call to a cardinal. Besides, she'd have her own
day at court soon enough, when she became a great healer in
her own right. Wasn't Nathan always comparing her to Trotula,
the famous woman physician who wrote medical treatises and
taught at the university in Salerno? "You see?" he would say
to Zarah. "She's another 'Dame Trot'!" Grandmère would
always just shake her head.

Her reasoning had worked, it seemed. There were no demons
in Grandmère's kitchen. Breathing deeply to calm her nerves,
Leah noticed that her grandmother had ceased her plucking and
was squinting at her in the darkness, waiting for her to continue.

"No doubt Father will cure both the cardinal and his physician at once," Leah remarked, a bit hysterically. "They will
see how brilliant he is, and reward him. And he'll teach me
his arts, and I'll become a great doctor as well, and travel
the world!"

Grandmère Zarah was not to be fooled; something must have happened today. Leah was on the verge of tears.

"So, we're no longer in love?" she prodded gently. "Ah, well, it is probably for the best. First choices are always bad luck, you know. Did I ever tell you about the first suitor my father picked for me?"

Leah shook her head and bit her lip.

"His name was Samson," Zarah intoned ponderously. "He was so handsome! He was a good deal older than I, with a deep voice and a big beard, so manly and sophisticated!" She sighed girlishly. "I thought I was in love! How I cried when I learned he was to marry another! He was betrothed to Jobine de Troyes, who was rich and plump, before my father could come up with a bride price. That's because Samson was arrogant, he wanted a fortune!" Grandmère Zarah laughed, waving the partridge, now fully plucked, over the table. "Luckily, it turned out, because just two years later, he was so much older, his ears drooped from his head like wings and his teeth dropped like petals. He grew fat!" Zarah held the back of her hand over her mouth and dropped her voice to a whisper. "And his smell was very bad!"

Zarah hooted to herself as she felt around the wooden table for a paring knife. Leah began to laugh too. The light came back into her eyes and she felt a rush of warmth for her grandmother. Zarah hadn't demanded to know where she'd been or reprimanded her for running off in the morning. The loss of her vision must be frightening, yet she never complained.

"But you know, child, these men are not all so bad," Zarah concluded. "Look at your grandfather, rest his soul, and your father. Soon we'll find you a good husband, and you'll be happy."

Leah felt her face flushing red and her temper rising, suddenly uncontrollable. "I don't want any husband!" she screamed at Grandmère. Toppling her bench, she heaved a turnip to the floor and stormed from the room, aching from the strain of the day, frightened of demons, mourning the loss of her first love. In the heavy silence of her father's workroom, Leah was overcome with shame at her outburst. What could have come over her to shriek at Grandmère that way? Zarah's story had been meant to cheer her. She just didn't understand, that was all.

Filled with remorse, Leah returned to the kitchen. It had grown late. Zarah had finished preparing the partridge and was absently stirring the kettle on the hearth.

"Grandmère, I'm so sorry," Leah said, retrieving her bruised turnip. "I meant no disrespect."

"We'll talk more some other time," Grandmère Zarah said quietly. "Now ready the supper things, for I hear your father's footsteps outside, and it sounds as though he is bringing some-one with him."

Chapter
4

Scorpio had not ventured far into the forest before his fear and exhaustion all but dissolved. In their place he felt a confidence and energy that seemed to come from somewhere beyond him. From beyond him, yes— but from somewhere within him as well. *The orb?* The question formed in his mind, and as quickly disappeared. Traveling in the direction the girl had run, he made his way through the green woodland with a sense of calm that was enlivened by moments of pure rapture; for he was enchanted with the beauty of the unknown planet on which he had landed.

He had never imagined an interplanetary journey before, though of course he knew it was an everyday occurrence for the Hunter folk and their many visitors. His own people rarely left their aquaglobes and hydrogardens. How limiting, he thought. This was exhilarating! Everything was new. Already he had noted several kinds of songbird, and a few small mammals and insects. These he found interesting. But the variety of vegetable life filled him with reverence. There were so many strange species! And the forest through which he was passing seemed to have developed at random, obedient only to its own forest laws—unlike the strictly ordered and painstakingly cultivated plant life on Terrapin. Here were pines and oaks, shrubs of myrtle, lowly ferns, ancient trees and slender saplings, all growing companionably in one place!

Scorpio sighed. Much as he loved his homeland, its liquid gardens and its water-filled globes, there was a familiarity to this foreign wilderness that pained him. Had Terrapin been

like this once, before the Hunters? Scorpio suddenly knew that
it had. He knew it with a certainty he had no need to question,
and the knowledge made him heartsick. How could his people
have forgotten how they once lived? How long had it been
since the wildlife on Terrapin was truly wild? Since the fish
had been permitted to breed freely, the mammals to mate un-
watched, the plants to root where they may?

He must tell them on Terrapin. He must remind his people
of the old ways.

In the relative safety of a grove of trees, Scorpio removed
the darkened orb from his sleeve, turning it, prodding it gently,
studying its marbleized skin. "Take me to Terrapin," he willed
it, resting a hand on its leathery surface. He concentrated, he
spoke the words aloud, he prayed. But the orb appeared to
slumber, its inner light dormant, its mysteries sealed within.

Scorpio was forced to give up. *Water*, demanded his brain
with a primal urgency. His senses were alert to the sound of
it, the smell of it. Drawn to a cool running brook, he bathed
and drank his fill, and emerged refreshed, the water streaming
from his limbs in sparkling ribbons. His cetaceous skin was
once again glossy and soon paled to a mottled ivory beneath
the Benedictine habit. The scratchy garment, bloused at the
waist and secured with its knotted cord, afforded a pocket where
the orb could rest. There the dim ball, held snugly against the
cavity of flesh beneath his rib cage, generated a cosy warmth.

He would have to find help to master its powers. With renewed resolve, Scorpio continued on his way to the city, de-
scending a hillside when the forest thinned. At the foot of the
hill, a man-made orchard of olives and figs marched away in
tidy ranks that seemed almost homelike after the undisciplined
forest. There was no one in sight between the neat rows of
trees. Drawn by a strong smell of water, Scorpio aimed east-
ward and soon emerged on an unpaved road that bordered the
western bank of the Rhône. The breadth of the river took his
breath away. And with the recognition of unlimited water there
came joy. He would not have to worry about lack of moisture,
that was certain.

Alert! Scorpio drew back into the orchard. There were travelers on the road. Moving toward him, two couples led primitive wooden carts drawn by stocky beasts. It was the custom
of these people to be clothed, he could see. The men wore

knee-length tunics and thick leggings, leather boots, and loose hoods that bunched into cowls around their shoulders. Their wives wore simple dresses with the hems tucked up at the waist to reveal contrasting underskirts of gold or blue, and head-coverings of plain white cloth. The men walked together in weary silence, while the women trudged behind, talking in high, flat voices, like the girl Leah's.

Following some distance behind the couples was a trio of men, all with a curious circle of fur circling their bald heads, dressed in brown frocks not unlike Scorpio's own. Their voices were lower. From the safety of the orchard, Scorpio studied their slow but steady progress, their hooded heads angled downward, their arms crossed in front of them, their hands invisible, each hidden away in the opposite sleeve.

The travelers all walked in the same direction. Scorpio looked to the north. On the horizon he could see a stone bridge that split the sparkling river like the scalloped fin of some mammoth silver fish. On the east bank, blurred by distance as though it were under water, a city like a crowded reef climbed a rocky hillside. Houses roofed with rounded clay tiles, red, brown, orange, clustered together like so many snails, and gray stone buildings clung to the rock like barnacles. Barely visible, topping the craggy mound like a colony of sea urchins, was the largest building of all, a pale stone palace with crenellated turrets and two piercing spires.

Avignon, thought Scorpio. The home of the girl Leah, and the dwelling place of the supreme ruler of this world, the Pope. The watery image of the city in the distance pleased him.

In imitation of the travelers he had seen, Scorpio pushed his hands into the sleeves of his habit and emerged onto the road with his eyes cast downward. The posture had its merits. With his arms crossed before him, he could both support and conceal the bulge of the orb at his belly. His peripheral vision suffered with the peaked cowl pulled forward, but his face was fully shadowed. Taking slow, measured steps, he fell into line with the traffic, too far from his fellows for conversation, but close enough to avoid a conspicuous solitude.

Scorpio attracted little notice on St.-Bénézet's Bridge; travelers in clerical garb were by no means uncommon. So far he had seen only one species of cognizant, though they varied greatly in detail. There was a marked diversity of physical

stature—in this, they were more like the Hunters than his own
people—as well as differences in costume and coloration. They
were quite noisy. And their odors were strong: heady, or perfumed, or foul. Many of the men had hair growing from their
faces as well as from their heads. All of them had the same
formation of cheek and nose as had Leah, the same outlined
mouth and lidded eyes. Scorpio found them rather awful—and
so, presumably, they would find him. It was no wonder that
Leah had been alarmed.

By the time Scorpio reached the gatehouse, Avignon loomed
invitingly ahead and the Palace of the Popes was a crisp sil-
houette against the evening sky. His quest for help was almost
at an end. Once off the bridge, the palace couldn't be more
than a few minutes' walk away. Scorpio patted the orb at his
belly, looking for all the world like a roly-poly friar who had
just had a full meal. He started for the gate. But a problem
presented itself. People were offering small bits of metal to the
gatekeeper, some sort of coinage, it appeared.

Scorpio backed away from the gate, searching for a quiet
place to consider his plight. He paused at St.-Bénézet's Chapel,
a small stone building with a vaulted ceiling that was built onto
the bridge, supported by one of the pilings. Just beyond the
chapel was a group of men who appeared to have stopped for
a rest. Two of them were lying on the cobblestones. They were
all variant types, Scorpio noticed. There was a man with only
one leg, and another with bandaged eyes, and yet a third, made
crooked by a hump on his back, who supported himself on
crutches and held out a quavering hand to passersby.

Squatting gratefully a short distance from the hunchback,
Scorpio could watch the travelers line up at the gatehouse to
pay their tolls. He could jump into the river and swim to shore,
that was one solution. But he would certainly be noticed. And
he didn't want to risk harming the orb. It was growing darker.
Perhaps a wooden cart would join the line; he could cling to
the rear, or conceal himself inside. Searching the distance, he
thought he could see a wagon or two making their way across
the bridge. He would just have to wait.

A shadow fell over him. "Do you need help, Brother?"
asked a voice. Forgetting himself, Scorpio looked up, directly
into the face of a black-robed monk who had just finished his

evening prayers at the chapel. As their eyes made contact, the monk recoiled. Then, gesturing quickly from head to chest to shoulders and muttering wildly, he hurried away. Scorpio drew the hood of his garment further forward and hung his head. His face frightened and repulsed these people, of that he no longer had any doubt.

Behind him, the hunchback brandished a crutch and called out angrily, "Begone, interloper!" But Scorpio was oblivious to the threat. The shadow was back. Scorpio watched the hem of the black garment as it brushed the ground before him, but he did not look up again. "God be with you, Brother," said the voice. A coin dropped into Scorpio's palm, and the black robe hastened away, murmuring, "Have mercy on his pitiable soul. . . ."

Scorpio suspected he had been the object of charity. Turning the coin over in his hand, he silently thanked the Deity for using his plight to provoke a blessing from the black-gowned man. For were not acts of kindness a balm to the soul? Perhaps there were more similarities between his own people and these long-robed folk than met the eye. With his faith renewed and strengthened, Scorpio waited for the monk to disappear, then hurried through the gate to Avignon.

Behind him, the hunchback adjusted the ball of rags strapped between his shoulder blades and breathed a sigh of relief. "Who let that leper among us?" he demanded of his companions. "Even the truly blind and legless couldn't compete with that. Why, he was as wasted as Lazarus himself!"

Scorpio had found little to complain of on this new planet—until he encountered the overpowering stench of Avignon. So much compost going to waste! There it was, clogging the riverbanks, floating in roadside gutters, fertilizing cobbles and brick. But, Deity be thanked, even the smell worked to his advantage. For just as few residents ventured far without a cloth of some kind to cover their mouths and noses, so Scorpio could walk with his head erect, eyes exposed, though shadowed, holding the roomy cowl across his face.

The city struck him as both quaint and forbidding. Most of the dwellings were single-storied, though crammed together along muddy streets. Everything was made of wood or stone. There was no noise from pumps or generators, and none of the piercing metallic whirs of Terrapin's industrial centers; but the river roared and people shouted, cart wheels trundled through cobbled alleyways, and the din was as ferocious as any Hunter stronghold.

Overlooking it all, the Palace of the Popes topped the gray stone boulder on which it was built like a bronze crown on a dowager queen. Hugely scaled, with walls nine feet thick and towers some 150 feet high, it dwarfed the little houses that proliferated in its shadow with barely an alley's width to separate them. The facade was so plain as to be almost barbaric, broken only by the narrowest of windows, peaked and trefoiled in the Gothic style, and by two slender spires that framed the main gate like devil's horns, the sole ornaments on an otherwise impenetrable exterior. The gate itself, a cavernous opening, was the height of three men, carved and arched and guarded by men-at-arms.

Scorpio tried to squelch a wave of dread as his mind spewed forth the image of Chanamek. For a moment he could almost see it superimposed on the Papal Palace, an implacable steel ziggurat with a soaring central tower and corona of snoutlike telescopes that continually searched the night. The Palace of the Popes was primitive by comparison, though no less imposing. It was not the home of a man with no enemies, Scorpio reflected, but rather the citadel of one who commanded all the power in his realm, and yet feared to lose it. This was a fortress, built to endure. Like Chanamek.

For all its austerity—and unlike the Hunter citadel—the Pope's palace seemed open to any and all who wished to enter. A constant and varied stream of people disappeared through the gate, among them, Scorpio noticed, several men wearing light-colored habits very like his own. Even as he spied on the fortress in the gathering darkness, two boys in matching livery emerged to light torches against the evening's gloom. The orange firelight reflected dully in the chain-mail armor of the palace guards, who stood at attention as yet another lively crowd passed through the gate. There were no coins exchanged that Scorpio could see. No one was questioned, no one turned away.

Emboldened by his observations, Scorpio adjusted his copious hood, placed a steadying hand on the orb at his waist and, trailing a boisterous knight and his squire, walked quickly be-

tween the unflinching guards into a dim vaulted passage beyond
the gate.

In a burst of torchlight at the end of the passage, the Palace
square opened to the night sky, bounded on all sides by stark,
soaring walls. But within the walls, the enormous courtyard
was a pool of color. Guests posed or strolled in merry groups,
sporting a rainbow of finery, trimmed with wafting plumes and
fluffy furs, yards of silk or filmy gauze. Here and there a figure
in a pearl-white robe would move through the company like
an egret among peacocks. To the right, musicians ringed a
large stone well. To the left, like a fountain, a wide stone ramp
overflowed with courtiers whose voices swelled above the
strains of song and festive laughter that drifted to the courtyard
from some inner banqueting-place.

Scorpio, undaunted, threaded his way among scurrying servants and chattering courtiers, up the ramp and through another
gaping arch, to the north wing of the palace. The spill of guests
thinned to a trickle for the length of a lofty, pillared promenade
with a massive wood-beamed ceiling. One side of the promenade opened to an unlit cloister, its thick low hedges lending
texture to the blackness. At first glance, Scorpio thought the
cloister deserted. But as he followed the walkway, he gradually
became aware of muffled whispers and mysterious squeals emanating from the hedgerows. High above the cloister, from a
brilliantly lit second-story gallery, banqueters leaned through
pointed windows, hooting at the figures hidden below.

Was it a game? Were they watching his progress as well?
Scorpio nervously hugged the shadows, his confidence beginning to wane. Images of the Hunter stronghold flicked at his
memory, accompanied by faint impulses: *Run! Flee!* Rounding
a corner, he gasped in fright; an equally startled pair of lovers
popped apart at his approach. Averting his face, he hurried on,
wondering at the choked guffaw that followed him. "Good
evening, Brother," called the young man, hushing his para-
mour, who had dissolved in a rippling peal of giggles.

Scorpio's confusion mounted. Did the beings taunt him? Had
they recognized him as an outsider? They couldn't have seen
his face. But perhaps his behavior was incorrect. Had he vi-
olated a custom? His black-robed benefactor on the bridge had

also called him "Brother," he recalled. Next time, he would reply to this greeting in kind.

Scorpio paused to collect himself at the foot of an immense staircase. But his mind still churned out haunting images of Chanamek, and his sense of foreboding increased. He had found his way to another mighty fortress; but who were its architects, if not crude giants? There was, as yet, no sign of an advanced technology, no evidence that any of the cosmic energies had been harnessed, no indication that interplanetary travel was practiced. Nor had he seen representatives of other cognizant species. Although the girl Leah had distinguished her own people from those ruled by the Pope, the distinction seemed to be merely tribal.

Could he expect these beings to accept his presence, understand his tragedy? Come to his aid? What if they feared him, just as his own people in their aboriginal tales, centuries old now, had feared the developing Hunters? Would this Pope be a leader wise enough to have intuited truths beyond his species' present capabilities, that there existed other beings, other worlds? And what world had he come to, where was he? Where Terrapin?

Scorpio was panicking. His mind issued orders to *breathe*. *The orb!* He groped for the orb; it had slipped forward over his belt and pulled at his front like a pendulous tumor. Breathing deeply and cradling the orb beneath his habit, tightening his belt and securing it in place, Scorpio struggled to regain his focus. How easy it was to lose track of his purpose. His imagination had gotten the better of him; but the plight of his people had to be his primary concern. For now, the orb had not yielded its mysteries. His next hope was to find Pope Clement VI.

Scorpio proceeded up the broad staircase, attracting little notice among the clusters of guests who conversed on the landings. The young lovers he had disturbed scampered past him hand in hand, not giving him a second look.

He emerged before a crowd of revelers who filled the colonnaded loggia that overlooked the cloister far below. Both the surge of guests and a lilting music seemed to originate from a doorway midway down the corridor. Over the throaty voice of a perfumed and buxom lady of the court, Scorpio could distinguish the tinkling of crystal and the clanging of platters, the odors of roasted meats and wine.

"It's too tragic," the young woman asserted, waving a ring-laden hand in a mink-trimmed sleeve. Her golden hair, bound in a silken net, was held in place by a simple jeweled fillet from which fluttered a lacy veil. "He is the cardinal I most favor. So cultivated and kind. It was his heart, they say. You should have seen him, the poor man! He was as green as the *sauce verte*."

"Let us pray he recovers, Lady Isabeau," said her companion, a stout auburn-haired lady encased in brocades, whose large rolled headdress was spotted with pearls. "He must be strong of heart. For it's said the Cardinal de Gascon is as generous as he is kind." She raised an insinuating eyebrow.

"Oh, he is, madam," said Lady Isabeau sweetly. "*Very* generous. Second only to the Pope himself!" She coughed slightly, then added gravely, "As befits his station, of course."

All at once a strident fanfare was sounded and cymbals clanged. The guests began to herd toward the doorway at the center of the corridor. One red-faced gentleman lurched the wrong way, halting to clasp the pudgy hand of Lady Isabeau's companion.

"Clement VI lays a fine table," he announced, jovially slurring his words, "but I'd rather romp with you, my pheasant, than taste the sweetest of subtleties!" He stooped unsteadily to kiss her hand.

"You'll have to romp alone," the lady replied, snatching her hand away, "for I'm returning to the Grand Tinel. The next course is about to begin, and its subtleties are a fairer attraction than you, sir! Why, the Pope has promised a miracle!"

Scorpio followed the two ladies excitedly. He was learning much from their conversation. A cardinal, it seemed, was second-in-command to the Pope. And the Pope performed miracles to entertain his guests!

The Grand Tinel, as he expected, was a mammoth dining hall, five times longer than it was wide, paved with stone and hung with paintings and tapestries. The ceiling, barrel-vaulted for its wondrous length, was covered in blue fabric studded with golden stars, and soared as high as a Hunter launching silo. Many of the decorations showed figures with golden discs behind their heads. Could they represent orbs? Perhaps these people did know of interplanetary travel—was it possible?

Increasingly jostled by the crowd, Scorpio trailed the ladies around the perimeter of the immense hall. The lengths of the Grand Tinel were lined with guests' tables that stretched from a raised dais at one short end to an overflowing sideboard at the other.

Some of the servants at the sideboard—carvers of meats and panters who sliced trenchers of bread, the almoner who kept the crusts and the servers who delivered the delicacies—were dressed in light-colored robes like his own. But all of them bore a knife or a platter, a ewer or tureen; Scorpio, empty-handed, noticed he was out of place at the end of the room closest to the dais, where the two ladies settled into their seats. Bowing his head even further and securing a place against the wall behind them, he searched for a break in the traffic so he could slide back to the great open door.

"It's a shame the Pope has retired to his quarters before the subtleties he planned," said Lady Isabeau as, with a flurry of trumpets, a stream of servants marched from the kitchen four abreast, bearing enormous confections of bread and sugar in lively colors, cleverly constructed in the shapes of entertainers, a juggler and a dancing bear, musicians and jesters. The guests oohed and gasped, laughed and applauded as figure after figure was paraded the length of the great hall.

Lady Isabeau's doughy companion squealed with delight at the sight of the edible sculptures. "It is a shame," she agreed. "No doubt he was very shaken by the illness of Arnaud de Gascon. These are the most magnificent of subtleties! It is truly a miracle what can be created out of simple sugar and paste. My mouth waters at the sight of that marzipan knight! Is he not handsome?" She tittered flirtatiously.

"On the contrary, my mouth has gone rather dry," Lady Isabeau replied, evidently bored. "You, there, butler—" She waved a hand at Scorpio.

Scorpio started in surprise.

"Butler, please see that our wine ewer is refilled," she continued, thrusting an elaborate silver pitcher backward over her shoulder, not bothering to look in his direction. "Just take it, there's no need to come all the way around," she remarked, then turned languidly back to her conversation.

Grabbing the ewer by its single, ornate handle, Scorpio took the opportunity to escape the banquet. He had no wish to be discovered as an imposter. Exiting the Grand Tinel, he chided himself for expecting a miracle of an interstellar nature! Clearly, he had allowed his hopes to lead him astray. Correcting his course, he set off in search of the Pope's private quarters. If this palace adhered to the logic of a Hunter citadel, the Pope would surely occupy a tower. The largest tower was at the opposite corner of the cloister, clearly visible through the openings in the colonnaded loggia.

Retracing his steps, Scorpio descended the grand staircase and crossed the darkened cloister garden. Opening a door in the base of the corner tower, he once again began to climb. A stone ceiling spiraled above him, supported by bleached bonelike ribs. The only light was afforded by torches, and the stairwell smelled of smoke and oil. Emerging at the top, he was in yet another long, narrow corridor that led to another, and another. The corridors were all of stone, some of them guarded by sleepy men-at-arms, others cold and deserted. Scorpio avoided the guards and wandered, searching for an unguarded doorway, perhaps a service entrance, that would lead him to the papal quarters. But it was difficult to distinguish one corridor from any other in this mazelike fortress, and he soon found himself, he thought, back in the hallway at the top of the stairs.

The corridor was interrupted at intervals by heavy wooden doors, arched and pointed, all identical. Scorpio was halfway down the hall when one of the doors behind him creaked open. He drew back against the wall as an elderly, white-robed monk exited the chamber nearest him and glided away in the direction of the tower stairs, his leather sandals swishing on the smooth stone floor.

Through the open doorway, Scorpio could hear snatches of a heated conversation.

"He can't last much longer," said a man's voice, silky and reassuring.

"We must pray he recovers," another said solemnly.

"Who's to say if this physician will be able to save him?" squeaked a third, agitated voice. "What if—"

"Our own Gisnard de Carliac has drunk himself into a stupor!" the first speaker interrupted. "We've fetched the nearest doctor we could find, the most famous physician in the Jewish quarter—and they're all renowned, as you well know." An imposing man, clean-shaven, wearing a bloodred robe, poked his head out of the doorway and called sharply to the monk, who had almost reached the staircase.

"Brother Celestine! Make haste with that water the physician asked for—His Eminence is failing fast!"

The voice was that of the first speaker. Scorpio froze, hoping he would be camouflaged against the ivory-colored stone. But the elderly monk must have spotted the glints of light on the silver ewer Scorpio still carried, and beckoned urgently.

"Hurry with that water, Brother," he hissed. "Didn't you hear Cardinal Signac? His Eminence the Cardinal de Gascon is dying! In here!" The monk disappeared into the chamber closest to the staircase.

Scorpio hesitated. He peered into the ewer. It held but a few drops of red wine. *Run! Flee!* cried his senses. But he would have to pass both chambers to reach the staircase to the cloister.

The ancient monk beckoned again from the sickroom. "What is keeping you, Brother? *Hurry!*" he croaked insistently. His eyes had widened in panic, but not, Scorpio thought, from the sight of an alien face. He doubted Brother Celestine had even registered his features. Something else had frightened him, something in the dying man's chamber.

Scorpio slid past the chamber in which the cardinal called Signac spoke with his associates. A glimpse inside revealed a cluster of figures, all in red. He continued stealthily to the sickroom door.

Suddenly two figures emerged. One was the elderly monk, his hood pushed back from a wrinkled scalp, his sleeves rolled up to his bony elbows, his face pale. The other was a middle-aged man in a flowing gown of dark red, with undersleeves of indigo and a black headdress made from yards of wrapped cloth. His trim, pointed beard was brown, as were his calm hands, compared to the monk's white, clammy forearms.

"The Cardinal Arnaud de Gascon is dying," said the doctor, clasping the monk's arm gently. "He's been poisoned. I've done all I know to do. You must fetch your superiors to administer the last rites."

Brother Celestine nodded weakly as the doctor returned to his patient. "You keep watch here until I return with Cardinal Signac," he ordered Scorpio numbly, "and ask the doctor if he still needs the water." He shuffled slowly down the hall.

Scorpio peeked into the sickroom. It was a small chamber, dominated by a narrow bed. Arnaud de Gascon, the dying cardinal, was lying on his back, straining to breathe with horrifying whimpers, his lips curled back from his teeth in pain. His unfocused eyes stared blindly at the ceiling. Pasty and sunken against the vivid scarlet of his gown, his face was twisted, though the muscles appeared to be frozen in place and his expression did not change. The exhausted doctor stood by the bedside, helplessly awaiting the inevitable.

Scorpio's mental messages had taken an uncharacteristic, though no less compelling turn. *Help him!* his mind cried. *Heal!*

The physician barely took his eyes from the patient as Scorpio entered the chamber.

"Take his hand and pray for him, Brother," he said quietly. "You can do little else, for he is fast dying. He has been purged and bled as well, but the poison was strong, and paralysis sets in. Soon it will reach his heart, and he will be free of his pain."

The physician stepped back as Scorpio approached the cardinal's bedside and leaned over the dying man. Arnaud de Gascon showed no reaction.

"He is blind," added the doctor. "It always goes thus with aconite. It is close to the end."

Turn him on his stomach, press the small of his back, came the unfamiliar messages. An irregular, rattling noise began in the cardinal's throat, and his face began to turn a sickly purple.

"Please allow me," Scorpio said to the doctor, dropping the ewer to the floor. "We do it this way where I come from." Grasping the cardinal by the shoulders and heaving mightily, he rolled him onto his belly so his face, now deepening to fuchsia, hung over one side of the bed. In a single, forceful movement, Scorpio threw his weight onto the cardinal's back and pushed.

Suddenly Scorpio felt a tingling heat beneath his ribs, as though the orb, secured beneath his robe, had become a living, moving thing. *The orb!* The messages must have come from the orb!

The sensations of heat and movement intensified as Scorpio pressed the hidden globe to the base of the cardinal's spine. It felt liquid, like a globe filled with water, but fiery, like the sun.

The doctor stood nearby, too stunned to protest, as the cardinal stirred and groaned. The dying man's lungs began to swell and his limbs to tremble. With a tremendous gathering of force, his head lifting, his eyes near to popping, he suddenly seemed to explode, expelling the contents of his stomach through his mouth, sending the foul matter fully across the small bedchamber. His body twitched, then relaxed to a calm, regular breathing.

Scorpio, who had struggled to maintain his position on top of the bucking cardinal, relaxed as well. As the heat from the orb abated, he climbed down from the bed and gently rolled the patient onto his back again. The cardinal's eyelids fluttered shut, and he slept peacefully, his face a slightly flushed but healthy pink.

Scorpio was well pleased. The orb had many powers, it seemed. It must have repaired his wounds from the Hunter laserfire, and now it had healed the cardinal as well. But had it responded to the cardinal's need? Or to Scorpio's empathy on seeing the cardinal in pain? And how had it engineered the messages he had received? Thus preoccupied, it took him several moments to notice the speechless physician, who was staring at him with a mixture of wonder and fright.

"Who are you?" he finally whispered. "And how . . . ?"

Run! Flee! Scorpio, alarmed, heard the approach of the other cardinals in the hallway. He mustn't be trapped here with the orb. This time he would obey his instincts. *Go!*

"Farewell, Doctor, a blessing on you and your patient," he blurted, and bolted from the bedchamber to the stairway, through the cloister, and down the monstrous corridor to the palace courtyard, where he concealed himself, breathless, behind the great stone well, his search for the Pope temporarily suspended.

In the bedchamber of Arnaud de Gascon, the Jewish physician, Nathan de Bernay, was trying to hush the incredulous cardinals as they crowded around the sleeping man's bed. In the putrid-smelling corner, a saintly Brother Celestine set to work with a bucket and scrub brush.

"You are a talented doctor indeed!" remarked one of the prelates, a short man with a squeaky voice. The others added their accolades.

"Cardinal de Laval, I thank you," said Nathan, "But I beg

you, allow the patient to sleep. The poison has taken a great toll on his energies, and he must rest.''

"Poison? Preposterous!'' said Bertrand Signac angrily. "Who would dare to poison a cardinal? Doctor, you are undoubtedly a fine physician, but it is obvious that this man is the picture of health. He has had nothing more than a touch of indigestion.''

Nathan de Bernay let the cardinal's protest pass. He had no wish to involve himself in the politics of the Papal Palace, nor did he care to tangle with Bertrand Signac, whose machinations were known to encompass more territory than the Pope's own, whose control had infiltrated the lives of kings and commoners alike, whose power had extended from Naples to Britain, from Spain to the kingdoms of the East, and whose displeasure was to be feared.

"Naturally, I give only my opinion, sir," said Nathan respectfully. "Perhaps I am mistaken.''

"Undoubtedly,'' answered Signac. "There must be no talk of poison!'' His voice took on a silken tone. "We don't want to panic several hundred banqueters!'' He chuckled as if the entire idea was ridiculous. The other cardinals tittered nervously in agreement.

"Indigestion!'' the Cardinal de Laval summarized the matter.

"The cardinal's health is restored," said Nathan, "and that is all that is important. But you must thank one of your own brothers for his help—for it was the strange Benedictine who healed the cardinal, even as he lay on the brink of death. Who is he—the deformed one? And where did he go? I would like to confer with him, for he has studied techinques I have never seen, and surely he has the healing touch! He left this ewer. . . .''

Cardinal Signac snatched the silver ewer from the doctor's hand and strode from the chamber, just in time to see the hem of an ivory-colored habit disappear down the great stairway.

"Brother Celestine!'' The elderly monk reappeared in the corridor, holding a bucket and scrub brush at arm's length. "Who was the brother who fetched the water?'' demanded Signac.

"I don't know, Your Éminence.'' Brother Celestine bit his lip. "I've never seen him before.''

"Well, find him and bring him to me!" Signac commanded, shoving the ewer at the trembling monk. "He dropped this vessel, perhaps he's returned to his service at the banquet. Go *now*!"

Nathan de Bernay exited the bedchamber with the other cardinals, closing the door behind him.

"I'll take my leave now, my lords," he said firmly. "The Cardinal de Gascon should be given milk and honey when he wakes, to soothe his stomach. His diet should be mild. Just the blandest of cakes, perhaps. I am gratified he lives."

"As are we all, Doctor," said Bertrand Signac graciously.

"Where are you, Brother? Cardinal Signac calls for you!"

Scorpio cowered behind the well as the elderly monk breathlessly crossed the courtyard, the silver ewer dangling against his pale habit. Brother Celestine shuffled painfully to the gate and searched the darkness beyond the palace, then returned to the courtyard and sighed. The crowd had thinned, but music and laughter still echoed from the Grand Tinel, less dense but increasingly raucous as the last of the banqueters drank and reveled into the night. From the shadows a nobleman and his lady staggered across the courtyard and out the gate. "All those stairs," the old monk whined tiredly. Then, resigned, he set off once again for the great banquet hall.

Scorpio waited for several minutes, until he was sure the monk had gone, then emerged from his hiding place.

"There you are, Brother!"

It was the Jewish physician. *Flee!*

"Please don't run away—I only want to thank you for your help. You are a great healer! Do you not know that Cardinal Signac seeks you? Why do you hide from a fellow member of your order?"

"I am not what I seem," replied Scorpio cautiously. The doctor's voice was warm and kind, and Scorpio's fear abated.

"Do you mean that you are not really a Christian brother?" asked Nathan.

"I am not," Scorpio admitted. "But I seek the Pope. I must see him."

"I understand," said Nathan sympathetically. He felt a wave of pity for the courageous stranger. What an odd, warbly speech he had. The poor man must have lived his entire life as an outcast, due to his terrible deformity. Probably he hoped that Clement VI could cure him. Was it leprosy? Or a defect of birth? Nathan would have to examine him at closer range to be certain.

"I am not sure that the Pope can work the miracle you seek," he said gently. "But *you*—you are a most talented healer. Are you from an Arab land? Would you could teach me your methods. I have studied with Arab physicians myself, you know, though never have I seen such a cure! But come. You will be in danger if you are discovered in the palace, impersonating a Christian brother. Perhaps you can arrange for an audience with the Pope on one of your feast days. In the meantime, why not stay with me? I have need of an assistant, and I can offer you shelter where you will find some degree of acceptance."

Scorpio was in no position to refuse help now that it was offered. But how could the physician know what he sought from the Pope? Was it a miracle he needed?

It felt as though eons had passed since his ordeal on Terrapin. The orb had cooled, and dragged heavily against his robe. Too tired to think clearly any longer, he gratefully followed Nathan through the Papal Palace gate, and then through the gate of the Jewish quarter. Soon he could sleep.

Chapter 5

"*My* house is yours." Nathan de Bernay ushered Scorpio into his cosy study and consulting room. He stowed his leather bag of tools and preparations in a wooden cupboard and lit a lamp with the candle that had been left burning to welcome him home. "Please rest yourself while I inform my mother and my daughter that I've brought a guest."

Scorpio waited patiently, glad of a few moments alone. The room was simple and pleasant, and sized at a comfortable scale compared to the Pope's palace.

Nathan went to the kitchen where Leah ladled an aromatic stew from the hearth and Grandmère Zarah was adding an extra place at the table.

"I see you have heard the tread of my guest!" said Nathan heartily. "I am sure you will enjoy him. I know little of the young man myself, except that he is a great healer, from foreign parts. Unfortunately, he has suffered some sort of calamity and his face is much deformed. Not the leprosy, so I judge, have no fear. But though he is not a Christian brother, he wears the garb of a monk to allow him free passage and to conveniently hide his face. His knowledge is uncanny! Tonight he cured the Cardinal Arnaud de Gascon of a deadly poison—indeed he brought him back from the very brink of death. I have asked him to stay with us for a while, and work as my assistant."

"Father!" Leah's outburst was pained and indignant.

"Leah, I am hoping to relieve you of some of the burdens you carry," said Nathan gently. "This way you will be able to study and help me at home, and aid your grandmother as well. You are needed here. Soon you will marry. . . ." At Leah's stricken look, Nathan broke off. "We will discuss the arrangement later, daughter," he continued. "You, too, will be able to learn much from our guest—more than I could teach you alone! So be kind to him, for his road has been an arduous one."

"I will, Father," Leah promised. How generous of spirit was her beloved father. She could refuse him nothing. But she was not about to be replaced by a stranger, nor would she agree to remain always at home while this mysterious young man traveled freely with her father.

Nathan disappeared into his study for a moment, and returned proudly, leading a slight, hooded figure.

"May I present Master Scorpio," he said. "Scorpio, my mother Zarah, and my daughter Leah."

Grandmère Zarah beamed delightedly at the newcomer and bade him sit down, warm himself at the fire, take a meal. She could just make out his shape, a milky figure in a peaked hood. She couldn't see if he was ugly—but that would be just as well if they were to have a young man living under the same roof as Leah. She was thrilled that Nathan had found a new assistant. At last he was coming to his senses! Now she could concentrate on finding her granddaughter a husband.

Leah felt faint and her mouth hung slack. Her father had brought the demon into their house, to live with them, he'd said! She couldn't wrench her eyes from Scorpio's face. He was staring at her with those wide, buglike eyes of his, and his lipless mouth had opened like a slash, then closed again in a short, tight seam. Why, if she didn't know better, she would swear he was as surprised as she! What kind of trickery was this? What did he want with her, with her family? Did he plan to harm them? Had she brought him forth? And what was he doing disguised as a Benedictine, of all things?

"Try not to stare, Leah, it's rude," Nathan whispered, seating Scorpio across from his daughter. He passed a bowl of scented water, that all might cleanse their hands. He said a brief blessing, and insisted on serving his guest himself. "This young man is a miracle worker," he told Zarah enthusiastically, serving Scorpio a portion of turnips.

Of course he works miracles—he's a demon! Leah's thoughts

were racing. Her father seemed so happy. How could he be so impressed?

Nathan continued to chat graciously, occasionally shooting his daughter an encouraging glance. But Leah, wavering between terror and guilt, anxiously prodded her food. Periodically she would glare at Scorpio, willing him to return to his own demonic realm. But the creature refused to meet her eyes, and at length began to eat as though he hadn't seen food for days.

Grandmère Zarah was gratified to see her supper so enthusiastically consumed. The young stranger was attentive, too, and she hadn't felt so amusing in years. She told several cheerful stories of her youth, and found the newcomer's rippling voice to be soothing and pleasant. But how silent Leah is, she thought. Could her granddaughter be attracted to this quiet young man? Or is she finally learning the proper modesty for a young girl? Either option would be satisfactory, of course. All in all, Zarah could not have been more pleased.

As Leah numbly cleared the remains of the dinner from the table, Nathan relaxed and spoke of his days at university. There was something about the young stranger that made him feel nostalgic for his youth. Zarah had felt it too, he noticed. But his guest was painfully self-conscious and reserved. Probably he was not accustomed to feeling accepted. They must all do their best to make him feel at home.

Scorpio was worried about the girl Leah, who seemed about to explode with tension. That she feared him was clear, but he hoped she would soon understand that he meant no harm. Warmed by the hearthlight and stimulated by the fragrant smell of stewed herbs, he found himself deeply interested in the lives of this close-knit hairy family. It was a privilege to dine with them, he felt, for who else among the Aquay had ever supped with another species? Although he was careful to keep his remarks to a minimum, he responded gratefully to their kindnesses and stories, and, as the girl stayed silent, he began to eat hungrily. He listened to the doctor's tales, and finally a sleepiness stole over him that even the orb, nestled warmly at his belly, couldn't dispel.

Nathan yawned, as did Grandmère Zarah. Leah glowered at the demon with narrowed eyes.

"Fix Scorpio a pallet in my study," Nathan bid his daughter. "It seems we all need our beds."

"I will see to our guest." Leah uttered the first words she had spoken since the demon had come into her house. She had never felt more enervated, sapped of all strength and reason. Fear propelled her as she waited for her father and grandmother to retire. Fear and fury. She would have to keep her voice down, for her father would still be awake and at his prayers. She whirled accusingly on Scorpio.

"You were supposed to possess Aimeric, not me," she hissed. "What are you doing here? Why do you torment me? You cannot stay—I will tell them you are a demon, and no physician! Why, you are not even powerful, you told me so yourself. What trick did you perform and call a miracle to seduce my father? Do not think that you will seduce *me*!"

Scorpio roused himself to confront the troublesome girl. What must he do to soothe her fears?

"I performed no miracle, it is true," he said wearily. He raised beseeching eyes to the girl's angry face. "Please listen, for I tell you the truth. Have no fear of me. I am not a demon. But neither am I of your world. I am simply a lost traveler from a galaxy distant from yours." He paused and sighed. The girl was staring at him blankly. "Yours is not the only planet that is populated with beings who can speak and think. You will have to use your imagination to understand. Think of me as a foreigner from an undiscovered land, if you will."

Leah regarded the demon skeptically. Were there madmen among demons? Perhaps he had been expelled from his own world, perhaps he was a demon with delusions. But he spoke as guilelessly as a child, and seemed neither evil nor dangerous. And he had healed a man.

The orb.

"It was not I who healed that man."

The demon had spoken as though he could read her thoughts. Leah suddenly pictured something, something she had dreamt, perhaps, a ball of light.

"It was this—it was the orb,"

Briefly turning his back on Leah, Scorpio withdrew the instrument from beneath his robe and held it forth for her to examine once again. The orb glowed dully. Leah cracked a shy childlike smile, as if greeting a well-loved, but distant, memory.

"You know I seek to discover its powers, to learn how it

works. Tonight I sought the Pope, not your father. We met only by chance. It may have been the orb that led me to the sick man, I do not know. But I learned that it can heal.''

As it had in the field, Leah's mood again mellowed as she watched the orb, its faint orange light slowly swirling, warming her complexion and the demon's like a fading fire. From upstairs, her father's pious chanting reached the study. She felt protected by his prayer. Maybe this is all a dream, thought Leah finally. I must sleep.

''Please, I must sleep.''

There, that was the proof. Leah was startled from her reverie. The demon echoed her thoughts, he must be of her own creation. But how to explain the compelling and glorious mystery, the orb? Probably it was nothing but a bladder with a candle inside, a cheap magician's trick.

''I must conceal the orb in a safe place,'' said Scorpio. ''Your father has never seen it, nor has any other. Only you. Will you help me to hide it? Just for this night. Then I will be gone. Please, for I must rest.''

Leah was too confused to fight any longer. The creature seemed genuinely weak, more tired even than she. Well, even magicians and madmen had to sleep. ''I will help you hide your magic globe for one night,'' she conceded, ''and tomorrow you will go. We suffer no demons on the Sabbath. Do you agree?''

Scorpio nodded. Leah led him to a large ebony chest. Beneath the carved lid, a deep tray was filled with the drying herbs she had gathered that morning. As lovingly as one might cradle an infant, Scorpio laid the orb amongst the herbs and closed the chest. Then, as Leah departed, he spread his blanket on the deep red carpet and slept.

Leah's fear of the demon had abated. He had made no move to touch her. Surely he would not come near the bed she shared with her grandmother. He seemed to want only shelter, for the present. But she could allow no harm to come to her family. If she did conjure him, she must also watch him. Skirting the stairwell for the blackness of the kitchen, she lit a candle and settled down at the empty table, a troubled, wakeful guard.

● ● ●

The candle guttered and Leah jolted awake. It was not yet dawn. She had better get to bed before Grandmère Zarah discovered she had spent the night in the kitchen. She tiptoed toward the stairwell. A sickening memory of the previous night's dinner crept over her. Had the nightmare been real?

In the dim light of her flickering taper, she could see the figure of the demon magician huddled on her father's prized carpet. Stealthily, silently, she moved to the herb chest and cracked the ebony lid. A golden glow suffused the room and a fresh, spicy aroma wafted from the chest. In the colors of spring, green and violet and buttery yellow, her herbs had started to flower.

Chapter
6

*B*efore breakfast on the morning of the Sabbath, Nathan de Bernay cheerfully gathered his family together and attended services at the synagogue. Scorpio had declined to accompany them as Nathan's guest, saying that there was something he must do. Nathan was secretly disappointed. He would have liked to show off his new assistant and introduce him to the community. But he understood. Scorpio would not be comfortable as a center of attention.

It was unfortunate, Nathan thought. Such a fascinating young man, though full of contradictions. Scorpio was a puzzle, to be sure. For one thing, he claimed to be widely traveled. But his grasp of geography seemed to Nathan to be rather fuzzy. And while he said he had never taken religious vows, yet he appeared to own nothing but the threadbare Benedictine habit he wore. He seemed to have a vast knowledge of plant lore, judging from the little conversation they'd enjoyed last night. Scorpio had listened with great interest as Nathan described the symptoms of aconite poisoning he had observed in Cardinal de Gascon. But the few plants Scorpio had mentioned Nathan had never heard of. They must be terribly obscure. Exotic.

Come to think of it, Nathan never did quite pinpoint where Scorpio had come from, or where he had studied medicine. He only had the sense that it must be unimaginably far away— Cathay, perhaps? Would Scorpio be an idolator, then? Nathan did find it curious that one with such a seemingly empirical turn of mind would fall prey to superstition where his own misfortune was concerned—did he truly believe the Pope could cure him? But perhaps in Scorpio's situation, one would try anything, cling to any hope. Such a horrible deformity. What could the Creator have been thinking of?

Nathan, catching himself, silently apologized to God for doubting His wisdom. Sighing reverently, he fastened his eyes on the conical glass lamp that burned perpetually before the holy ark and rejoined the men at their prayers, calling the responses he had committed to heart since his boyhood.

From behind the wooden grille that screened the narrow women's section from the rest of the temple, Leah listened to the service with her eyes tightly closed, fervently praying that the demon be removed from their midst. But she soon found it difficult to concentrate.

"They say he is stern, and also spoiled," whispered a voice next to her.

"Silly, you will soon cure him of that! Now find one for me!"

"There he is! Can you see him?"

"I think he's handsome—how lucky you are!"

It was Félicie and Jacobine Morel. They were discussing the various attributes of Daniel, the rabbi's son, who was to wed Jacobine. The bride-to-be was peering through the latticework and studying the boy's every move with an intensity he must have found unnerving, for now and then he would look over his shoulder as though he knew he was being watched.

Grandmère Zarah leaned across Leah's shoulder to shush the two girls. But she smiled tolerantly, and shot Leah a meaningful look, as if to say that the synagogue was as good a place as any to shop for a husband.

Leah rolled her eyes and looked disgusted. She had spied through the wooden slats many a time, and knew what she would see: the same boring boys she had grown up with, surreptitiously scratching their backsides or wiping their noses, lost in prayer or shifting from one foot to another, it didn't matter. There wasn't one she would care to take for a husband.

Leah tried to fasten her mind on worship. But thoughts of Scorpio intruded, intertwined with an angry vision of Aimeric de la Val d'Ouvèze. She was amazed to realize that she hadn't given Aimeric a thought since the demon's arrival last night. She was strangely grateful for the respite. Now that she really

considered it, the demon had done no real harm. So far he had
provided her with the courage to face up to Aimeric, and he
had helped her father to heal an important official at the papal
court. She had no doubt that the orb was something special;
not after seeing her neatly tied bunches of wilting herbs revived
as though she had placed them in water. Magician or madman,
monster or monk? If he disappeared as he'd promised, she
might never know. And if he was a demon—well, she decided
he must be a good demon, after all.

Scorpio needed to find a hiding place for the orb. He had
seen the look of wonder on Leah's face when, in the darkness
of pre-dawn, she had lifted the lid of the herb chest and gazed
at its spectral light, how the light of understanding had dawned
in her eyes. Early this morning, Scorpio himself had gazed
with a mixture of horror and awe at the budding blossoms and
newborn florets on the marjoram and lavender, savory and sage.
It was wearying to be the custodian of such power. It would
be better if the orb was hidden until he could find someone to
help him use it well.

He had promised Leah he would leave her house once he
was rested, and although her father had been generous and
kind, Scorpio would soon be called upon to explain his miraculous medical techniques. It would be best if he left. He
would search for a hiding place where he could come and go,
someplace that reminded him of home. Later he would return
to thank Nathan and Zarah, and to bid Leah farewell.

Thus resolved, Scorpio set off for the river. But suddenly
changing his mind, he set off for the palace first. If he did get
to see the Pope, he would want to have swift access to the orb.
Perhaps the well in the courtyard would do?

Much to his disappointment, the great openwork gate to the
palace was shut, as was a wooden barrier behind it. Scorpio
could hear men's voices, droning together in a low and hollow
chant that echoed from somewhere beyond the walls. He followed the sound along the narrow alley that fronted the palace,
uphill to the source of the song.

The voices were coming from Notre-Dame-des-Doms, the
huge cathedral that flanked the Papal Palace. Scorpio had noticed the building earlier, because its slender belfry almost
matched the height of the Pope's greatest tower. But beyond

the cathedral was something he hadn't noticed: a garden.

Drawn to the greenery, Scorpio climbed a steep embankment and found himself in a vast park on the palace grounds, high atop a rocky hill. Up here, the wind was crisp and cold. All of Avignon stretched below him, the flat blue ribbon of the Rhône, and the undulating sea of houses, jammed together in crooked rows and roofed in rippling tiles of red and rust. Up here, above the city, were the barns and the henyards, the orchards and vegetable gardens that supplied the Pope's table. Here Scorpio felt almost at peace.

Scattered throughout the park, workers, male and female, weeded flower beds and planted seedlings, tended animals and pruned shrubbery, as deer and peacocks roamed freely among the trees. Here and there a gardener in tunic and breeches would look up from his work to wonder why a thin Benedictine brother had chosen to skip his morning's prayers and wander in the garden. But most found it no mystery.

Scorpio watched one of the workers, a portly man in a hood and leather apron, as he strode purposefully to a well-trodden path and disappeared, whistling tunelessly, into the trees. He had been carrying an implement that was strangely familiar, though long obsolete on Terrapin. It was a sort of mesh bag, fastened to a long pole. A net.

The path led, as Scorpio had hoped, to an oblong pool set among slender trees. A fishpond. The workman skillfully swept his pole through the waters, and departed with a thrashing netful of silver.

Peering over the edge of the pond, Scorpio longed to join the variety of fish within. The water was clear, but the pond was deep and lined with weeds; he could not see to the bottom. It was perfect. He released the orb from the confinement of his robe and tenderly dropped it into the water. There the orb floated for a moment, a summery golden yellow, then drifted to the center of the pool and gently sank.

The service was over and, as was usual on the Sabbath, Nathan was hungry for his breakfast. Joining Leah and Grand-mère Zarah outside the synagogue, he was proud to lead his two ladies homeward, one on each arm.

The de Bernays were surprised to find the door to Nathan's

study ajar when they arrived home. Who would disturb them on the Sabbath?

"Perhaps our guest has returned from his errand," said Nathan hopefully. It would be pleasant to talk with him over a long morning meal.

As they entered the consulting room, an agitated papal messenger jumped to his feet.

"Excuse me for intruding, sir," he said. "But you are the physician, Nathan de Bernay?" At the doctor's nod, he continued. "It's the cardinal, sir. Arnaud de Gascon. He's taken ill again, sir, and my master asks that you come right away."

"It is my Sabbath day, as you know," said Nathan politely. "But I will send my new assistant—he tended your master last night, and cured him well. Scorpio!"

"I'll look for him, Father," said Leah, hurrying to the kitchen, and checking the rooms upstairs. On her return to the study, she quickly peeked into the herb chest. The orb was gone. He had kept his word. "Scorpio has gone, Father," she said softly, relieved.

"My master asked for you, sir," the messenger persisted. "He said to fetch the Jew physician, Nathan de Bernay."

Nathan frowned. This messenger did not wear the arms of Arnaud de Gascon. "Your master—do you wear the livery of Bertrand Signac?"

The messenger nodded nervously. "He said it was most urgent."

"Is his own physician still indisposed, then?"

The messenger wiped sweaty palms on his haunches, still nodding.

Nathan sighed. "Very well. Cardinal de Gascon is now one of my patients, and I must go. Daughter, fetch my bag from the cupboard."

Leah regarded her father oddly. Couldn't he see that his bag was sitting in plain view, right on the table?

But Nathan was preoccupied. He had no love for Bertrand Signac, and it was well known that Cardinal Signac had no love for the Jews of Avignon. Nor did he wish to be involved with a poisoning. And Nathan was certain that de Gascon had suffered from aconite ingestion, for the symptoms were unique. The old Benedictine who had tended him, Brother Celestine, had reported the cardinal's alarm at the tingling in his body, and the distinct feeling that his hands were made of fur. By the time Nathan had arrived, de Gascon was racked with agonizing pains in the head and chest. He complained that his vision was souring, that everything was turning a yellowish green. And then he had descended into delirium and blindness.

Nathan had never known anyone with symptoms so advanced to be cured. By all of the laws of nature, paralysis should have stopped the cardinal's breathing and arrested his heart. If it hadn't been for Scorpio—where was Scorpio? Could he heal a dying cardinal twice?

Nathan pushed aside his trepidation. Probably de Gascon was only suffering from minor complications following his ordeal. It would be only natural. And if the symptoms were the same as last evening's, Nathan could turn him on his stomach and imitate the maneuver that Scorpio had used.

"Shall I go with you to the palace?" Leah asked eagerly, handing her father his bag. What was wrong? Her father seemed so troubled.

"Not on the Sabbath, Leah," said Nathan shortly. "And certainly not to tend to a cardinal. I want you to wait here for Scorpio, and if he returns, tell him what has happened. It is his help I might need."

Leah nodded. Her father thought he needed Scorpio, but what he really needed was the magical ball. And now she had sent Scorpio away. Well, it was all for the best. Father was the finest doctor in Avignon, with or without that orb. And of course her father was right, a cardinal's bedside was no place for her. She was sure the cardinal would recover. Father would become a famous healer at the palace, and . . . Would she ever get to see the inside of the Papal Palace?

As Nathan hurried into the bright Sabbath morning with the messenger, Leah comforted Grandmère Zarah, who had fallen to trembling, though she couldn't say why.

Chapter
7

Arnaud de Gascon was already dead, and had been so for well over an hour, Nathan judged. Even from several yards away, at the entrance to the small bedchamber, he could see that the pupils were fixed and dilated, the mouth motionless and slack, the skin a pallid gray. About the eyes, though they may have been blind before the end, there remained a suggestion of terror, as if to say, "Lord, no, not this again."

On either side of the narrow bed, long-faced cardinals stood solemnly over the corpse as Bertrand Signac completed the rite of extreme unction, dipping his thumb into a small pot of waxy balm, anointing the forehead, closing the eyes, marking the ears, nostrils, lips, hands and feet of the deceased, asking for absolution of his sins.

Nathan bowed his head respectfully for the duration of the sacrament; the room filled with the sickly sweet odor of the balm.

"I regret to see that I have arrived too late to be of service," he said when the ministrations had ended. "Please accept my condolences."

"You hardly look surprised, Doctor," said Bertrand Signac. The malice in his tone was unmistakable. Slowly wiping his oily thumb on the inside of one scarlet sleeve, he challenged Nathan de Bernay. "Do you suppose this to be another case of poisoning?"

"Has he eaten or taken any fluids?"

"He seemed well this morning," a quavering voice piped

65

up. The tremulous speaker was Brother Celestine, the elderly monk who had attended de Gascon so faithfully the day before. "He was exhausted, but cheerful, and woke at dawn. He took tea and a little cake—a poppy seed cake, his favorite, specially prepared for him this morning. I took it in to him myself and—"

"Silence!" ordered Signac. "I would hear what our famous physician has to say."

Nathan, taken aback at Cardinal Signac's vehemence, was nonetheless reflecting on the similarity between poppy seeds and the tiny seeds of *Aconitum napellus*: monkshood. Still, he couldn't be sure that a second dose had been administered to the deceased.

"His first ordeal left him in a greatly weakened condition," he ventured cautiously. "It's possible that, as a result, his heart has failed. If you'll allow me . . ."

"Don't let him touch the body!" Signac commanded.

Nathan jumped backward, startled, and collided with the messenger, who blocked the doorway.

"*You* are responsible for the death of our lamented cardinal, Arnaud de Gascon!" Signac lowered an accusatory finger at Nathan. "Do not try to deny your guilt—yesterday's 'miracle cure' was just a ruse, was it not? An excuse to plant *this*!"

Reaching under the pillow of the dead cardinal, Signac extracted a reddish object, which he held up to a stunned group of cardinals, then brandished in the incredulous face of Nathan de Bernay.

It was a wax doll, crude and lumpish, with the crown of its head flattened into the shape of a cardinal's hat. Through its heart was a single bronze pin.

"Last night you planted *this* in his bed!" Signac cried triumphantly.

Nathan was reeling from outrage and shock. The heat in the small room and the overpowering smell of the sacramental balm were making him nauseous. He breathed slowly to steady his temper, all the while chiding himself for having broken the Sabbath.

"It's the same kind of doll you Jews make. We know about your invidious sorcery! Why, a Jewish doll like this one was once used in a plot to murder the Pope himself!" Signac was raving. The shortest prelate, Cardinal de Laval, looked at Nathan with a combination of disgust and fear. The expressions on the faces of the other cardinals ranged from doubt to boredom.

"May I examine the doll, if you please," requested Nathan quietly. He turned the waxen image over in his hand, then nodded curtly and passed it back to Signac. "It is true that some of my people have made such dolls . . ."

"Aha!" shouted Signac.

". . . .but they are used only to divine the location of lost objects. I do not hold with such superstitions. I am a physician, sirs, and know nothing of sorcery. Furthermore, the plot against the Pope you speak of occurred over thirty years ago. You may recall that the dolls used against John XXII were made to order for one of your own bishops, who was later hanged!"

Signac bristled as several of his associates chorused their agreement that Nathan's memory was, indeed, correct.

Nathan's dignity had been restored. "I am an educated physician, a man of medicine," he asserted. "You called me in yourself. Why would I want to murder a cardinal, a man whom, until last night, I had never even met?"

The prelates nodded, and looked questioningly at Signac. The physician's reasoning was sound.

"Perhaps he owed money to one of your kind, eh? To one of your relatives?" Signac grew increasingly venomous.

"I assure you, that is not the case," replied Nathan.

"Then you deny the charge of murder by treachery?" cried Signac.

"Most certainly."

"Search his bag!"

A quartet of guards had materialized in the doorway. One of them stepped forward and emptied Nathan's leather bag on the cold stone floor. Surgeon's tools of iron and brass tumbled forth, clanking atop the soft packets of herbs. Small glass cups, used for bloodletting, clinked against the wooden boxes of salve. A bit of cloth drifted silently to the floor, a scrap of cloth that Nathan did not recognize. Signac bent down to pick it up, and withdrew, meticulously, ten tiny objects one by one, letting each fall to the floor with a metallic ping.

"You see, my lords," said the silky voice, "how the Jew carries with him brass pins?" He paused. Then shouted. "Pins! Like the needle that pierces the very heart of this waxen doll!"

Nathan's protests were ignored.

"I want this Jew's house searched for instruments of sorcery! Guards!" Signac was in his glory. "Take this self-styled physician to his dwelling place and conduct the search in his very sight!"

Signac had trapped him, whatever the reasons. Even had he kept the Sabbath, the outcome would have been the same, Nathan could see that now. Falling silent, he turned his thoughts to God.

Chapter
8

*S*corpio, unencumbered, slowly returned to the Jewish quarter from the palace gardens. His steps dragged, for without the orb he felt heavier rather than lighter, as though the force of gravity had increased, and his plan of action, conceived in optimism and previously so clear and simple, now seemed cloudy and full of holes.

The morning was warm, and the deep Benedictine hood was beginning to itch his head. How he wished he could move about freely, with his face turned to the sun. But so far Nathan and his sightless mother were the only beings he had encountered who didn't find him entirely repulsive. Nathan was tolerant and kind, Scorpio reflected, and he seemed to be a learned man. He decided to risk Leah's anger to speak to her father just once more, to learn what he could of this powerful Pope, and of the planet and its ways. It looked as though he might have to spend some days on this world, and he didn't even know its name.

No one stopped him at the gate in the rue Jacob, though a lone Benedictine was a less than common sight in the quarter. Everyone, including the gatekeepers, was hastening to the scene of a commotion in the public square before the synagogue. Scorpio stopped short. Nathan de Bernay was being marched through the square in the custody of eight armed guards.

Filled with confusion and horror, Scorpio stayed at the back of the crowd. What could this mean? Could it have anything to do with him?

"Stand back, on the orders of Cardinal Bertrand Signac!" the captain of the guards shouted, pushing at the crowd.

A tall, commanding man swept into the square. He wore a dark green overtunic, and his thick black hair and curly beard were both neatly parted in the middle. He was followed by several other men of similarly dignified appearance.

"I am Rabbi Isaac de Lunel," he announced to the guards. His tone was friendly, but firm. "Evidently you have made a mistake. Nathan de Bernay is a renowned physician and a most respected member of our community. It is unthinkable that he would commit any crime. I demand his release. Please ask Cardinal Signac to submit his complaint to my authority, and we shall certainly take action in our own court, as is our custom, if it has any merit."

"This exceeds your authority, Rabbi," replied the captain, an officious youth who was evidently much enjoying the proceeding. "The doctor is accused of murdering Cardinal Arnaud de Gascon, and we are ordered to search his house."

An outcry went up from the crowd as the guards dragged Nathan across the square in the direction of his house. Scorpio pushed forward. On the opposite side of the square, he could see Leah, a stricken look in her eyes, clutching her grandmother's arm and backing protectively toward their doorway.

"Go back to your houses," the guards shouted at the crowd. "Keep back! We won't tolerate any disorder in here!"

At the rabbi's signal, the crowd fell back and parted, creating a path to Nathan's door. Nathan turned, as though to reassure his neighbors. But his eyes suddenly locked with Scorpio's. Never had Scorpio received a clearer message. *Run! Hide! Now!* Scorpio obeyed, and ran from the quarter, his hood flapping loosely away from his face.

One of the guards, following Nathan's gaze, caught sight of the fleeing Benedictine. "Stop that monk!" he shouted, grabbing another of Signac's men and breaking into a run. "It's the Jew's accomplice! The leper! The Jew hired a leper to lay his hands on Arnaud de Gascon!" But somehow the crowd seemed to thicken around them, impeding their progress, and the mysterious monk vanished into the maze of alleys that was Avignon.

• • •

By the time the two guards returned to the house of Nathan de Bernay, bewildered, empty-handed and panting for breath, the search had turned up a cache of reddish wax and a crucifix belonging to the dead cardinal.

"You knew right where to look, didn't you? Your own messenger put them in the cupboard himself, this morning," Leah shrieked furiously at one of the guards. "He was sweaty and nervous, and now we see why. My father's bag was removed from the cupboard and left on the table. It was tampered with, can't you *see*?" She turned from one guard to the next, all of whom avoided her eyes with the exception of the young captain, who smirked.

With Leah wailing and Grandmère Zarah pleading piteously, Rabbi de Lunel trying to reason and the inhabitants of the Jewish Quarter heaving insults in their anger and outrage, Cardinal Signac's honor guard bore a quietly defiant Nathan off to prison.

Chapter
9

*P*ope Clement VI was enjoying fish for dinner again. The firm white flesh was moist and springy, and perfectly garnished with a syrup of ginger-spiced wine. The fish had been particularly abundant lately, according to his chief cook, and, Clement observed, unusually tasty as well. He must make a note to congratulate his kitchen staff.

How lovely it was to dine alone in the comfort of the papal apartments. Clement savored the last of his meal and called for a flagon of Châteauneuf, newly arrived from the papal vineyards north of Avignon, to be sent to his study. He moved from his private dining room through the robing room, where, for once, no ambassador awaited a private audience, no cardinal came to complain of another, no communication from the *camerarius,* the much-needed and equally dreaded minister of finance, urged him to curb his spending or threatened to disturb his sleep.

Clement exchanged his vestments for a nightgown and cap of whitest linen and a roomy, ermine-lined overrobe. His soft, pinkish skin thus swathed in white, his bald head safe beneath the prophylactic cap that outlined rosy cheeks, puffy eyelids and full, pursed lips, Clement resembled nothing if not a huge and sensuous infant, or perhaps the man in the moon.

Dismissing his chamberlains, he climbed the stairway to his bedchamber, which occupied the entire fourth story of the Magna Turris, the Great Tower. Here, more than anywhere else in his palace stronghold, Clement felt secure. The tower walls were ten feet thick, built to protect his holy person and, no less significantly, the library and two treasuries that sand-wiched his bedchamber. On the sixth story, some one hundred fifty feet above the Great Courtyard, sergeants-at-arms guarded the peace from a crenellated turret.

By day, Clement VI excelled in his role as Pope. His legal and political experience was as broad as his theological knowl-edge, for he had served as chancellor at the French court before advancing to a cardinalship. His eloquence was as renowned as his elegance. His court was magnificent and his expenditures lavish. He was a king of kings. But his duties were demanding and public. He reserved his nights for the enjoyment of the finer things.

From his bedchamber, the Pontiff followed a narrow con-necting passage to his study, a small room housed in a sec-ondary tower he'd had erected adjacent to the Magna Turris to expand his personal apartments. Above him was his private chapel; below, two stories of wardrobe rooms and, on the ground floor, a private steam bath of which Clement was righ-teously proud. But the study was his haven, and he looked forward to an evening of solitude, with no thoughts of the eternal squabbles between England and France or the trouble-some wars in the Papal States, no worries about his flagging plans for another Crusade, or this unfortunate business of Ar-naud de Gascon. Eagerly he anticipated the flavor of the full-bodied red wine, heady, like his reading, and warm going down.

Settling comfortably at his reading table, Clement wrapped a long but pudgy hand around the jeweled goblet that stood, brimful, waiting for him, and drank. There began the stirrings of profound satisfaction. He considered with ever-deepening pleasure the frescoes that adorned the study walls, frescoes he himself had commissioned as a respite from the scenes of angels and martyrdoms that covered the rest of the palace. Here were secular scenes of worldly delights, hunting and falconry, women bathing and children playing, scenes of forests, or-chards, birds and beasts, all on a background of rich dark green. At the top, a frieze of wildlife on a ground of red marched merrily beneath the wood-beamed ceiling that was itself cov-ered with patterns and florets. Only in the study, buried in the center of an impregnable tower, were the artworks peopled, not with saints, but with noblemen and servants gracefully engaged in outdoor pursuits, all painted to order for a Pope who was too often confined by his own enormous power.

Clement looked wistfully at a dreamy, yet animated scene of a brown-hooded hunter in a forest of evergreens, setting his ferret after a hare. Then his attention was captured by a portrait of the papal fishpond. The pool held all manner of swimming things, pike and carp, and ducks and a dolphin, while men at the water's edge fished with a long-handled net and a weighted cast net, and a hook and line. The scene, like the others in the study, had been painted by the court painter, Matteo Giovanetti di Viterbo. Ah, the Italians. Perhaps, thought Clement, pausing to drain his goblet, he should invite Matteo back to add more fish to the fishpond, considering their recent plenty.

Clement saw patronage of the arts and letters as one of the duties, and delights, of rulership. His mind on inspired Italians, he opened a volume he was curious to examine, an edition of new works by the diplomat and innovative poet Francesco Petrarch, recently returned to Avignon from his native Italy. Clement hoped to attract Petrarch to a position at court. The poet had already turned down an apostolic secretaryship, having no desire to be distracted from his writing, he claimed. Perhaps a bishopric? But Clement was aware that Petrarch found the court at Avignon to be corrupt, even dissolute. The Pope couldn't comprehend the poet's thinly veiled disgust. Petrarch simply refused to separate his vision of the papacy from the reality of Clement the man. But was the poet not a man of the world? No one had written of love of woman with more passion than he; he had worshipped his idealized Laura above all others, and his lines since she had been taken by the Black Death were nothing less than sublime.

> She used to let her golden hair fly free
> For the wind to toy and tangle and molest;
> Her eyes were brighter than the radiant west.
> (Seldom they shine so now.) I used to see
>
> Pity look out of those deep eyes on me.
> ("It was false pity," you would now protest.)
> I had love's tinder heaped within my breast;
> What wonder that the flame burned furiously?

She did not walk in any mortal way,
But with angelic progress; when she spoke,
Unearthly voices sang in unison.

She seemed divine among the dreary folk
Of earth. You say she is not so today?
Well, though the bow's unbent, the wound bleeds on.

The wound bleeds on. Sublime. Clement sighed. He couldn't help but think of Cécile, the raven-haired Countess of Turenne. Perhaps he should have invited her for the evening. She must visit again soon. Come to think of it, it was unfortunate that Petrarch had encountered the countess, dressed as a man, waiting to be admitted to the papal chambers. What thorns in the side these Italians could be to a French Pope! Take this matter of the strife between the Visconti of Milan and the Florentines! But as artists they were unsurpassed, such sentiment, such command of the lyrical. . . .

All the same, it had been a stunning disguise. Clever, even titillating. In truth, it disguised little. Emptying the flagon into his goblet, Clement let his thoughts drift back to the challenging advantages of the Countess of Turenne.

The very thought of her brought stars to his eyes. Clement VI pressed his eyelids to clear them of the oddly flickering lights that swam in his vision. Eyestrain, he didn't doubt, caused by reading with such concentration. As he blinked, the lights began to coalesce. The flickering steadied and leveled into two pinpoints of light that hovered near the ceiling. With them Clement could hear the murmur of voices, as though there were watchers in the rafters. Were there spies in the chapel above him?

"Guards!" called Clement assertively. But his command came out in a strangled cough, as, instantaneously, the lights grew blindingly bright, and two red devils popped into his study.

They wore long black gowns that fell from the shoulder, leaving their crimson arms bared. Their leather skullcaps were also black, with openings for two goatlike nubs on the forehead, and spiraling ram's horns that swept backward and pierced the air above their heads. Their faces were hideous, birdlike, with elliptical eyes as black as their gowns and a sweeping cheekbone that crossed from ear to ear, creating a beaklike point where the nose should be. One of the devils was large and well muscled, and exuded the cleverness and agile strength of some mountain-dwelling beast. The other was also tall but elastically thin, with a regal bearing and piercing stare. The thin one held a small glowing ball that swirled with golden light of a wondrous intensity.

Clement VI crossed himself repeatedly and recited prayers in Latin. He was stupefied, even frightened. But a good part of him was already dumbfounded by wine, and his own self-regard afforded him additional protection from stark terror. For who should have visions, if not the Pope? He was to be tempted, it was clear. The devils had probably divined his reverie about the Countess of Turenne. Perhaps it was a trifle immodest, perhaps—

"You are the leader here?" It was the thin one who spoke. His voice was reedy and resonant, like the sound of an organ as tenor notes issued from its pipes.

"I am Pope Clement VI, representative of Christ Our Lord on Earth." Clement replied with poise, then intoned: "I adjure thee, O serpents of old, by the Creator of the World who hath power to cast into Hell, that thou depart forthwith from this house, in the name of our Lord Jesus Christ, Amen!" Devils must be respected, of course, but one must hold one's own ground.

"We care nothing for your God. Our business is with you, Clement VI."

The Pope balanced slightly, but his voice remained firm. "You have come to tempt me, then? I will never succumb to your invitation to Hell!"

"We invite you nowhere."

The Hunter assassin spoke patiently. First encounters on new planets were always difficult. And he was pressed for time, so, perhaps unwisely, he had omitted the usual formalities.

"You are here to torment me, then," cried Clement, his mood abruptly conciliatory. "I confess my sins freely. For must we not sin to overcome sin? Must we not experience temptation in order to reject it?"

The two Hunters eyed one another sourly. Foreigners were so unpredictable.

"We did not come here to bargain," the assassin stated

flatly. "Listen closely, Clement VI. We are here to find another of our kind, an Aquay. He is bearing an orb, one of these."

Clement stared, mesmerized, as the devil held forth the beautiful ball. Light swirled about its surface like firesmoke.

"We know he has it, and we know he is nearby. He is called Scorpio. Do you know of him?"

Clement shook his head, distracted. What a curious thing was this ball of light. Could it be a trick of Satan's?

"I have never seen another like you, nor such a wonder as this orb," he replied. "What does it do?"

"It has many powers." The muscular devil seemed about to say more, but he was hushed by his companion, who withdrew to the corner of the study. There the two held a whispered consultation.

"He obviously knows nothing." Lethor the Assassin held the orb away from his body and noted the information relayed from the sensors at the front of his helmet. "There are more of these beings nearby, we must make haste now. Besides, my skin burns and pinches in this humidity. Scorpio must have buried the orb, or ours would have led us directly to it. Therefore, Ardon, we will have to track Scorpio himself."

"When we find him, Scorpio is mine," said Ardon the Stalker, flexing the scarlet skin that tightened over his biceps. "But we can use this Pope being to draw him out. He is the ruler of this planet, is he not? He must have a network of spies and informants like any leader."

"We must guard against the error that the Pope himself makes, Ardon," said Lethor. "We must not form conclusions based on our experience of our own world. We don't know the extent of his power, nor by what right he rules. Nevertheless, your idea has merit. For the Pope concludes that we have come to cause him torment, and we frighten him."

Clement VI felt annoyance bubbling inside him like an impending belch. How dare these devils consult behind his back!

"Return and face me!" he bellowed.

"Certainly," said Lethor, turning to the Pope. His tone was syrup, wicked. Brandishing the orb in the face of the astonished Clement, he hollered back. "You will search for Scorpio! He has stolen that which is ours! Use every means that is available to you, O Great One. For if you do not find Scorpio, we shall return to torment you. We shall cause you unending pain such as you have never known, nor can you imagine such torture. You have one week. If you fail to find Scorpio, your future is agony and anguish.''

Turning to face one another, the devils grasped the glowing ball of light between them and vanished.

Clement was spent. His hands trembled and his face was as white as his ermine robe. He clutched at his heart and searched the shadows. Could it have been the wine? He quickly regained his composure as four guards tromped into the room. It would be unseemly to appear so vulnerable in front of subordinates. What did they want? Had he called for them?

"We heard shouting, Your Eminence," said one. "As did the chamberlain working in the wardrobe beneath you. But it seems we were mistaken. Please excuse our intrusion."

"You saw nothing?" Clement asked, forcing a casual tone.

"No, Your Eminence. Nothing." The guards were obviously confused.

"You are very alert. For there was nothing there! I was rehearsing a sermon, and I am afraid I was carried away with my own oratory. But please, wait without until I dismiss you."

Clement moved to his spacious bedchamber. A fire crackled brightly in the hearth. But even with his guards posted just beyond the doors, even in the elegant turquoise chamber, painted with golden vines and arabesques, songbirds and squirrels, he no longer felt secure. Beneath the down-filled covers on his great bed, he resolved to examine his situation with as calm a wit as he could muster. Had the chamberlain and the guards heard the devils too, then? Or was it his own shouting they had heard? The creatures may have been real. Or they may have been a nightmare, brought on by thoughts of Petrarch and too much wine.

If he ordered a full-scale search for a devil, he would be thought mad. But what if this Scorpio was real? And what of the treasure the devils were after—what of the orb?

Clement was haunted by his vision of the orb. Could it be he had seen the Sacred Orb of the Pantocrator? Perhaps this Scorpio was the angel who controlled it. Perhaps with such power, no devil could harm him. Perhaps . . .

The connoisseur in Clement began to overshadow his fear, and even his awe. What a coup it would be to own such a relic. How he would like to procure such a piece! Not at the price of his eternal soul, of course. No, he would have to find this Scorpio and buy the orb outright.

The court illuminator, a weathered artist of advanced years, was up all night with an agitated Clement VI. By morning, he had produced a portrait of the devils the Pope claimed to have seen in a vision of Hell. One of the likenesses, a tall, thin, red devil, held a glowing ball of fiery orange.

Clement VI had pronounced himself well satisfied. He, too, had been awake until dawn, composing the sermon he intended to preach at the morning's High Mass at Notre-Dame-des-Doms, describing his terrible temptation, and how he had overcome it by shouting down the demons and invoking the Name of the Lord.

Quietly, but insistently, he had slipped the portrait of the devils, not yet dry, to a select few of his private guard, with orders that they should search far and wide for such a one, and bring him to the palace.

And, mad popes being no great rarity in anyone's experience, the guards had hurried off to do his bidding, no questions asked.

Chapter
10

*G*randmère Zarah perched stiffly in Nathan's narrow, straight-backed armchair, thin-lipped and silent. Leah bustled around her, sobbing mindlessly and picking through the disorder Cardinal Signac's men had left in their wake. Manuscripts and instruments were scattered across the floor, herbs and powders had been ground into the precious carpet, flasks were broken and liquids spilled. But the chaos was a needless blind, Leah knew. She had watched the captain of the guards signal his men to cease the wrecking. Then he had walked purposefully to the corner cupboard, wrenched it open and withdrew the evidence that damned her father.

"A crucifix, of all things!" she shouted bitterly. "What would a Jewish physician want with such a thing? How stupid it all is! It's just not fair!"

Zarah made no response. At last, overcome with frustration and misery, Leah threw herself at her grandmother's feet and whimpered, "Oh, Grandmère, why is this happening? Where have they taken him?"

And at last Zarah stirred from her chair. Pulling her shawl tightly around her shoulders, she drew herself to her feet and spoke with steady resolve. "Our people have long been persecuted," she told Leah. "We have been driven into exile and our temples have been destroyed. We have been named as witches, slaughtered and burned. Even here, in the safety of Avignon, we have been confined to this quarter and banned from the guilds. Perhaps it is God's will that our love for Him

80

be tested through trials that never change." She gripped her granddaughter's arm and fastened her dim eyes on Leah's own. "Heed me well, child. Your father is an innocent man. Like so many of our people who have gone before him, he has been falsely accused. But God's will will be done.

"I go now to find Rabbi de Lunel, to ask him to intercede for the life of my son. He will help us as best he is able. You, Leah, must put our house in order. You must pray to God that He imbue you with the dignity of Esther and the patience of Rachel. And tomorrow you will visit your father and find out what you may."

It seemed that all of Avignon was buzzing with talk of the Pope's morning sermon. People swarmed through every lane and alley, returning from High Mass at Notre-Dame-des-Doms. Gathering in groups of four or six, posing to show their Sunday garb to best advantage, they gossiped and speculated, expounded and twittered, as though they all had taken an excess of angelica. No one was discussing the death of Arnaud de Gascon, Leah noted wonderingly. Nor did she catch her father's name. How could they all go about their lives so blithely? Didn't they know that Nathan de Bernay was confined to a prison cell, accused of a sorcery? What could people be talking about that was more scandalous than murder?

Leah paused to eavesdrop on an agitated couple, perhaps a merchant and his wife.

"Only Pope Clement would banish not one but *two* devils from his sight!" said the man, a gaunt figure in a suit of russet and indigo. "I suppose he's seen the last of them!"

His wife, outfitted in saffron trimmed with vair, wrung her hands and searched the windows above the street. "We must be on the lookout for devils ourselves, he said. They come from above and appear when you least expect it. He said we are to appeal to him directly for salvation if we are visited. We must be ever vigilant, he said!"

The woman hurried into one of the choicer lanes of the city, pulling her husband after her.

More devils? thought Leah. Had Scorpio gotten in to see the Pope, after all? She had thought she was finally rid of him. But the merchant had said there were two devils. Were demons and devils the same? What if Scorpio was one of them? Could he be a Christian devil, after all? He had never seemed to be evil. He had even kept his word and disappeared the morning the cardinal died, just as he had promised.

Leah gasped aloud with the sudden realization: Scorpio could have murdered Arnaud de Gascon and implicated her father! Was it her own willfulness and disloyalty, then, that had brought disaster on her family? The thought was unbearable. She must find a way to save her father. Fervently she prayed to be granted all of the virtues of the matriarchs, Sarah, Rebekah, Rachel, and her namesake, Leah. Please, God, grant me the fortitude of Leah!

The dank prison was filled with drunkards and cutthroats of the worst sort. They jeered at Leah as she passed, their emaciated fingers wagging through small barred openings in heavy wooden portals. Nonplussed, an unkempt and unshaven gaoler conducted Leah to the end of a corridor.

"It's not often that we have a lady in here," he stated. "Your father's just around the corner. We kept him separate, you know, him being a sorcerer and all."

Leah opened her mouth to protest, but the gaoler held up an admonitory hand.

"Don't waste your breath, girl. I make no judgements one way or the other. I just lock them up, and sometimes I let them out. Here we are, then. I'll be back for you in a half hour's time."

Leah embraced her father, tears pooling in her eyes. She handed him his well-worn prayer shawl, and a loaf of bread, specially baked in the quarter in the great oven under the synagogue, that she had smuggled under her cloak. Aside from the dark circles that bespoke a sleepless night, he looked well enough. His mixture of joy and anguish at seeing her was evident.

"We have little time, daughter," Nathan began. "You must listen while I tell you what I know. My trouble is deep. For I believe it was Cardinal Bertrand Signac who had de Gascon killed.

"The night I was called to the palace, Signac had expected his own physician to attend. But Gisnard de Carliac was drunk. Perhaps it was Signac who made him so, to fog his judgement.

Or perhaps he would have lied on behalf of his patron, this I cannot know. But my colleague took too much wine and slept like the dead, and I was called in. The nearest Jew.'' Nathan paused to collect his thoughts.

"The poison causes heart failure, it is easy to mistake. But I had the misfortune to recognize the symptoms. I have no doubt it was aconite—monkshood. You know the plant?''

Leah nodded.

"I am not certain, but I believe de Gascon must have been given a second dose, perhaps on a poppy seed cake he took for his breakfast.''

Leah could hold her tongue no longer. "But, Father, could it not have been Scorpio who poisoned the cardinal, and allowed them to blame you? He was there, as were you. You know so little of him, after all. . . .''

"No, Leah,'' said Nathan firmly. "You must trust me and put such thoughts out of your mind. Scorpio is difficult to look at, I know, and a foreigner with mysterious ways. But he is a good man, a great healer, and we will need his help.''

"But—''

"Hear me out. The story becomes clear. Do you not know that the Pope is supposed to be at war with the Visconti family of Milan?''

"Those they call the 'Vipers of Milan'? But why—''

"The dispute is over territory in the Papal States. It is said that negotiations are under way for a treaty with Giovanni Visconti, the Archbishop of Milan. Such an alliance would replenish the papal coffers—Clement's treasury has dwindled and he borrows heavily to finance his wars and his lavish court. And you must know as well that such an alliance would replenish the fortunes of the cardinals, from whom he has borrowed, for they divide among them fully one half of the Church's revenues!''

"But I still don't see—''

"Now I shall tell you, daughter, that Arnaud de Gascon was known to be in the pay of the Florentines, the archenemies of the Visconti. De Gascon was working against the treaty, and he had Pope Clement's ear. While Signac, rumor has it, is nothing less than a Visconti spy.

"Arnaud de Gascon was meant to die the night I was called. But Scorpio healed him, and I was foolish enough to opine aloud that the cardinal had been poisoned. Signac had no choice but to do away with me and the cardinal both.''

"So Scorpio has done you harm!" Leah cried. "Oh, Father, I must tell you—"

"Scorpio has done no harm," said Nathan, shaking Leah by the shoulders. "They would have arrested me on the first night, had the cardinal died. My fate was sealed the moment I mentioned poison in the presence of Bertrand Signac.

"Listen, now, for our time is almost up. You, Leah, must find Scorpio and beg him for his help. You must search for evidence to clear my name. First, you must contrive to examine de Gascon's body and confirm that it was poison that killed him. Look for the seeds of the plant from which aconite is drawn.''

"Monkshood," said Leah, nodding. She had seen the plant with its purple bell-shaped flowers growing wild in the environs of Avignon.

"Perhaps, with your knowledge of herbs and Scorpio's knowledge of medicine, you will find a way to tie the poisoning to Signac. If you do, you must ask Scorpio to appeal to the Pope himself. In Christian law, the word of a Jew is never to be taken above that of a Christian. But Scorpio can speak in my defense. For he is not a Jew.''

Leah left the papal prison with an aching heart. She would carry out her father's wishes, of course. But no judge was likely to listen to a leprous-looking demon, Christian *or* Jew. Besides, she would have to find a hundred Christians to testify for her father to outweigh the word of Bertrand Signac. Leah beamed hopefully. What of her father's patients? How many of their lives had he saved? Surely they would do him this service.

She decided to pay a visit to her favorite patient, Mme. Roussillon. Hadn't she always been kind to Leah, and spoken to her of poetry and art as if to an equal, pressed upon her little books to read and encouraged her to broaden her interests? Surely such a cultured lady, with her passion for the chivalric ideals not just of courtly love, but of loyalty and justice, honor and truth and defense of the oppressed, would come to the aid of her esteemed physician, Nathan de Bernay. Mme. Roussillon would probably welcome the opportunity to offer Leah counsel, and might even contact her influential friends at court.

And if Aimeric was at home—Leah's stomach churned miserably at the thought—why, she would just ignore him.

Mme. Roussillon was embroidering linens in her small but elegant quarters. Her health appeared much improved, Leah observed. She stood and turned to receive Leah, and blinked with surprise, as if she were not sure whom she was addressing.

"It's Leah de Bernay, madame. The doctor's daughter."

Mme. Roussillon crossed herself rapidly and took a step backward.

"Well, so it is, and it's lovely to see you, my dear." Mme. Roussillon pressed a hand to her ample bosom. "You haven't brought more of the valerian decoction, I trust? For you can see, I am so much better now, and I hardly think I'll be needing . . ."

"I've come on behalf of my father," Leah interrupted.

"I quite understand that he won't keep our appointment, dear, you needn't have come. I was terribly shocked to hear what has befallen your poor father. Such a kind man, and an excellent physician. He must have been possessed by the Devil himself to have murdered a cardinal. I never would have thought . . ."

"Please, Mme. Roussillon, I have come to ask you—"

"Not after what has happened, I'm afraid. It would be quite out of the question." The matronly lady turned her back to Leah and wiped at her brow with a delicate linen square. "I'm just not looking for household help at the moment, dear, I'm sorry."

Leah choked back her anger and spoke steadily. "None of it is true, you know. He is no sorcerer, nor a murderer. You must know!"

But Mme. Roussillon had beckoned for her maidservant to show Leah the door. "You were always so like him," she muttered, backing toward her bedchamber. Her look held genuine pity, but it also held fear.

"Leah." The voice was soft, even sympathetic. So Aimeric had been at home. He must have followed her to the sheltered courtyard of his aunt's apartments, where Leah now stood, her shoulders slumped, her head bowed.

"How naive you are, after all." Aimeric was matter-of-fact. "It has nothing to do with the truth, you see. The situation is a matter of politics. Bernard Signac has found his scapegoat. What everyone knows to be true, none will speak. Not even I, should you grant me all your favors."

Leah shot him a furious glance. "You are all cowards," she hissed.

Aimeric shrugged, in no way insulted. "Cardinal Signac is a formidable enemy. My uncle, the bishop, fears him. Even the Pope would be wise to fear Signac." Grasping Leah by the shoulders, Aimeric gently lifted her chin so he could meet her eyes. "I have never meant you harm, Leah. Please believe that I am trying to help you now. And I am telling you that you'd best make your peace with your father."

Chapter
11

Leah's disappointment in Mme. Roussillon was as bitter as gentian; but Aimeric's dispassionate words held a ring of truth. She had tried to help her father in her own way, and it had not worked. Now she would respect his wishes. For it seemed there was no help for her father in this world.

Before the gates of the Jewish quarter were locked fast for the night, Leah slipped from her father's house. Embracing Grandmère Zarah at the threshold, she reassured the old woman that she was doing Nathan's bidding. Then, armed with a small oil lamp and a loaf of bread, she set off across the Pont d'Avignon to seek Scorpio.

Already there were stories being circulated in the quarter about the mysterious monk who had fled at Nathan's signal; of how the people had swarmed the cardinal's guards and allowed the stranger to escape; and how they had known him to be Nathan's new assistant, a foreigner of hideous aspect, but with unusual talent. He had not been seen since he disappeared into the rue Jacob. Leah prayed that he would have returned to the field where they had met.

Scorpio was her last chance. She knew not what he was, nor where he had come from. But she would appeal to him to help her: it was her father's will. Perhaps Scorpio could use his powers on Nathan's behalf—the powers hidden in the shining ball of light.

● ● ●

Deep in the darkening forest, Leah turned up the wick on her lamp and held it, swinging gently, at arm's length. Shadows danced around her like ghostly marionettes strung from twisted tree limbs. The night was cold, and the silence was deceptive, a velvety quietude brushed with little noises, close and subtle. Leah felt the nocturnal eyes of a thousand secret watchers; yet she had never felt more alone, as if she were the only living creature in an endless forest, and the rest of the world had disappeared.

With the descent of night, before the rising of the moon, the space around her seemed to thicken. Soon the yellow lamplight only served to render the blackness beyond its small aura all the blacker. Her crackling footfall sounded as loud as the din of the market at Prime. As she advanced, her presence seemed to generate a flurry of woodland night noise, hooting and scurrying, screeching and flapping. Leah's mind began to fill with images of spirits and demons, carnivorous beasts and birds of prey. Despite herself, she began to run, slowly at first, shielding her lamplight, and then more steadily, ignoring the brambles that pulled at her cloak, until she emerged, panting, at the edge of the fields of Montmajour Abbey and stopped short, witlessly dousing her carefully guarded wick in a single, violent sloshing of oil.

All it takes is a moment's negligence and the light can be lost forever. Leah sunk to her knees and wept, holding her face above the thin plume of smoke that snaked from the spout of the lamp. She wept in frustration and in despair; for fear of the dark and for love of her father. She cried in self-pity, and vowed to remain in place where she sat and never move again; and she cried for relief that the forest was behind her and now she could move on.

By the time Leah had done with her tears, the moon had risen, wrapping sky and earth in a wafting gray gauze. Leah ventured to the edge of the field, to the three stone gardener's huts where she had last seen Scorpio. The huts hunkered in the field like a row of sleeping bears. No movement came from within.

"*Scorpio!*" Leah whispered. No sound. Feeling for the cold stone openings, she whispered three times in succession. From each doorway, there came no reply, only the echo of desertion.

Leah tried again. She had been so sure she would find him here. This time she stood full in the doorway of each hut, searching the inky darkness for some sign of the demon or the glow of the orb.

This time she was rewarded. In the last hut she saw a shape, a patch of something less than black. Feeling her way in the darkness, knocking her shin against the edge of a wooden bench, Leah plucked at the warm scratchy softness of a Benedictine robe and tugged gently. "*Scorpio!*" But the empty garment came away from her hand and slid into a heap at her feet.

Bundling the habit under her arm, Leah strode purposefully back to the middle of the field. "Damn you, Aimeric de la Val d'Ouvèze!" she tried, stamping her foot. Scorpio did not appear.

All alone in the center of the field, Leah began to feel frightened again. The earth felt suddenly cold and damp. A layer of mist was beginning to form, blurring the edge of the world in reflected moonlight. On the farthest horizon, atop its craggy hill, the Abbey of Montmajour loomed, remote and spooky. Leah fell still, straining to identify the noises of the night. She realized that she had been listening all along to a sound that resonated from the trees behind the gardener's huts. It was a shrill, rhythmic chirping, multilayered, like the song of a hundred katydids. But it was much too cold for crickets. And there were variations in the sound, alternating with the chirping: two low warbling tones that overlapped like a hollow chord.

Despite her apprehension, Leah was drawn to the sound. She found it unlike any she had ever heard, and strangely beautiful.

Perhaps she had suspected all along that the source of the sound would be Scorpio. He had discarded his Benedictine robe and climbed into a tree, where, crouching low along a heavy limb, he raised his head to the stars and chanted. His coloring was dark and mottled. His huge eyes were open to the starlit sky, the brilliant moon reflected as a pinpoint in their midst. He made no sign that he was aware of Leah, and his chanting rose and fell.

Leah was frightened. Scorpio looked unhuman, like a salamander, or some tailless basilisk. But as she stood beneath him, silently awed, she was reminded more than anything of her father as his lips moved in candlelit solemnity, lost in prayer. Scorpio's song was such a reverie, comforting and sad. For the briefest of moments, Leah felt a stirring of mystical communion. Then, fearful, or perhaps unwilling to succumb, she withdrew from sight and waited for Scorpio at the base of a nearby tree, moved and lulled by his eerie song.

In the dead of night, Scorpio climbed down from the oak. Leah silently handed him his robe. Out of respect for the aftermath of prayer, she did not speak. Scorpio appeared to have found some comfort. But above all, Leah thought, he looked miserable and lost.

"Thank you," he said simply, and slipped into the robe. Almost immediately his skin began to pale. Leah, too, blanched as she watched the process.

"I have come on behalf of my father," she began, gathering her courage. "He is accused of murdering the cardinal you healed. We beg you to help us. If you have not the powers of a demon, perhaps your magical ball can help?" Scorpio listened, unblinking and still, fading from charcoal to smoke to an ashy gray to the palest eggshell brown. "Tell me again what you are," Leah whispered, "for you are so like us and yet so unlike us."

"I am of an outcast race on my own world," Scorpio began. "My home is called Terrapin, and we are known as the Aquay. My goal is to rescue my people from oppression and carnage, just as you now fight to save your father."

"There are outcasts even among demons, then?" Leah asked wonderingly.

Scorpio sighed. It mattered little what she called him, after all. It had taken courage for her to seek him out; he couldn't help but admire her for that. For the first time, albeit from need, she was willing to trust him. And she had requested, rather than demanded, his aid. Without the orb, he felt bereft, and in need of a friend on this backward planet. Maybe he and Leah could help one another.

"A demon I am not," he reiterated. "I am not yours to command, nor have you created me. But our paths continue to cross, it seems. So we must try to understand one another." The girl accepted this overture with a nod. But where to begin? "Tell me, Leah—what do outcasts do on your planet?"

If Leah was surprised by the question, she did not show it. She answered thoughtfully. "They band together, as have my people. Or they are doomed to wander alone."

"I am such a wanderer. It was the orb, you see. It carried me here—perhaps to you. Perhaps together we may find out why."

Leah looked confused, but she waited patiently for Scorpio to continue.

"The orbs have many powers," he explained slowly. "I don't yet understand how they work, or all that they can do. But I know that I somehow used the orb you have seen to travel to this place, and I believe it helped me to understand your speech. I know that it can heal, and we both know it helped your herbs to sprout."

"By magic?" ventured Leah timidly. So Scorpio had seen her in the study, after all.

"Does your sun shine by magic?"

"Not by magic, no. I believe that God has made it so."

"I don't know who or what created the orbs," said Scorpio. "But I believe they are more like little suns than like tools of magic. I think in some way they are of the natural world. Like the sun, they seem to have potential for great good, and also to do ill. But maybe they can be controlled by a master magician. Maybe they are magical, yes." Scorpio smiled ruefully. Despite his knowledge of interplanetary travel and hydroglobe technology, the power of the orbs seemed as magical to him as it must to Leah. But it occurred to him for the first time that perhaps the Hunters had not yet mastered all of the possibilities of the orbs. Did they know the orbs could heal? Scorpio wondered. Leah interrupted his thoughts.

"There are more than one of these orbs?"

"On Terrapin, there were three—three orbs." Scorpio's tone was musing and slow. "Our enemies, the Hunter folk, found one in their travels, then another and a third. Perhaps they used the first orb to lead them to the rest, I do not know. But the orbs embued the Hunters with overwhelming power. And they used this power to enslave the Aquay. Those who protested were slaughtered. They seemed to know the ones who would be driven to organize resistance."

The Aquay paused, then spoke with urgency. "They were going to kill me anyway, you see. They had murdered my friend. Leandro was his name." He met Leah's gaze. "That day, something inside me snapped. I chose, alone, to steal an orb and bring it to my kind. I thought with an orb I could restore some of the balance. But it has brought me here. Perhaps they will follow me, I don't know. I begin to weary of the chase."

Scorpio leaned against the massive oak and drew his knees to his chest.

"Who will follow you?" prodded Leah. "These Hunters?"

"Ardon," said Scorpio, a faraway tone overtaking his liquid voice. He closed his eyes.

Leah looked into his seamless, eyeless face.

"I must have angered Ardon," Scorpio said suddenly, emitting a bubbly rill.

Surprised and intrigued, Leah recognized the gargling sound as laughter.

"Something had snapped, you see. Leandro was gone and I was alone, poised at the edge of a solitary pool and ready to dive beneath the water, when I looked into the face of death itself: Ardon is his name. Tall and rugged. Handsome, even, as Hunters go. He squatted down and greeted me by name. 'Just a formality,' he said politely. 'The honorable Stalker always appears to his prey.'

"How fortunate for me, I thought, to have a Hunter *of honor* assigned to my personal execution. Is it preferable to be slain by a man of honor, do you suppose? But, after all, it was his honor that cost him his quarry—me! For the Aquay are good-mannered, and not likely to resist. So as expected, I nodded courteously and slipped meekly beneath the water. 'Until tomorrow, then,' he responded, and hunkered down at the edge of the pool to wait out the night.

"It was just as he expected. He planned to doze, and kill me in the morning. Until I slapped the water like a whalefin! Sent out a sheet of water like a wall of glass! Splashed him all over!"

Leah was taken aback. Scorpio was laughing, and could barely speak. As his watery peals grew stronger, their force almost tickled. Soon, she too was laughing until her eyes teared.

Scorpio struggled to regain control of his senses. He must have been very tired and overloaded for his brain to have triggered an emotional release of such force. *Laugh!* The command continued to squirt through his consciousness, and his body obliged. And now Leah was laughing too, with droplets running from her funny fringed eyes. How silly she looked, with her face so contorted. But her laughter was companionable and bubbly, and made him want to laugh all the more.

"B-but why is it so f-funny?" She managed to sputter. "He wanted to *kill* you!"

"It-it's the Hunters, you see," said Scorpio giddily. "They cannot tolerate the water, it burns them, and their skins shrink! But what's funny was, *oh, me*, it was his face! He was so surprised!"

They laughed until the convulsions wound down. Leah sobered first. She had earlier found release in a satisfying jag of crying. Scorpio soon followed suit. After his bout of laughter he felt energetic and cleansed. He was recalling the rest of his tale.

"I didn't stay to watch his skin turn red," he went on at length. "How he howled! It was a chilling sound, but I let him shriek. By the time I heard him blasting the water with his treacherous beam I was well away. And by then the next step seemed so simple. They were going to murder me anyway. So I stole into the stronghold of Chanamek, and I made off with the third orb."

Leah listened, rapt, as Scorpio described the terrors of Chanamek. He spoke of the Hunters, and of the Aquay and their ways. There was much she could not believe was true—Hunter weapons that shot forth beams of light, ships that traveled to the stars. Often, she told herself that Scorpio was mad, that he had dreamt a dream that he believed was true. But always she would remind herself that she, too, had seen the orb of light, and she, too, had witnessed its power.

As the night lifted to a pre-dawn gray, Leah gently interrupted.

"Scorpio, you have told me all I can comprehend in one night. But I must ask you—what has become of the orb?"

Scorpio sighed. Leah had been a patient listener. She had told him much as well. There were no other species of cognizants on this green planet. The people simply called their earth "earth." They knew nothing of its shape, or of its position in the galaxy. And he was still lost.

"The orb is hidden at the Palace of the Popes," he said. "I must return to Avignon to retrieve it. My quest is to master its secrets, and nothing less."

"But the cardinal's men hunt you in the city," said Leah anxiously. "And there has been more talk of devils—two devils. The Pope has vanquished them, it is said!"

Could the Hunters have come for him so soon? Scorpio wondered. How could they have found him? And had the Pope really bested them? If so, he was a powerful ruler indeed, and may yet be able to help. Maybe he should still consult the Pope. Or was this simply a superstitious land, ruled by sad tales of demons and sorcery?

"Scorpio, my people will protect you as best they are able. And I will help you to retrieve your orb, if you in turn will help me to prove the innocence of my father."

Scorpio found Leah's reaction to her father's imprisonment both poignant and practical. Nathan had been kind to him. And Leah had responded to his need with an offer of help, even as she had asked for his. "It is urgent that I find a way to return to Terrapin," he answered. "But if I cannot rescue my own kind at this moment, surely it is better that I detour for a short time to help another. I will do what I can."

Leah nodded and offered Scorpio a tired smile. "Even without your orb, you have special talents," she said. Scorpio acknowledged the irony with a watery trill. "I have thought very carefully," Leah continued, "and I believe I have a plan."

Chapter
12

*T*he sun rose, casting an autumnal orange glow over field and forest, like a low fire at the edge of the world. Leah was wide awake and filled with a hopeful excitement that overlaid her exhaustion from a sleepless night. She and Scorpio would save her father. She wanted to begin at once.

"I will tell you my plan on our way to Avignon," she said. "Let's be on our way, for the longer we delay, the more likely we are to be noticed by the brothers on the hill at Montmajour Abbey." Even as she spoke, the first faint intonations of the Benedictines at Prime carried across the valley. "If we are seen, they will think one of their novices has sneaked away to meet with a damsel near the gardener's huts, and send someone after us!"

Scorpio was able to laugh at Leah's little jest. The previous night she had explained to him something of the Church and its structure, and of the significance of the habit he was wearing. Despite his initial confusion, he was beginning to understand some of the complexities of earth society. There was such diversity, such a multitude of factions! One could be of the same race but of different nations; of the same nation but of different religions; of the same religion but of different races and nations. And the differences were so subtle! Physically, the people were all the same!

Among his own people there were differences in talent, in temperament, in personality. There was a class structure, to be sure. But the divisiveness on Terrapin was between the two species of cognizant, the Aquay and the Hunters. Their differences were clear; indeed, they were genetic! How could it be otherwise?

It would be amusing, Scorpio thought, if the squabbling earthlings had to cope with more than one species of humankind! As it was, they may as well have had dozens, considering the high seriousness with which they approached their differences. However, he reproached himself, it was absurd that he should be critical of a skirmishing planet, while full-scale genocide occurred on Terrapin. And he could little afford to indulge in nostalgia for the days when the two cognizant species on his own planet worked in symbiotic accord. He would do better to devote his attention to setting things right.

This morning, Scorpio too was filled with an energy born of renewed hope. He was eager to do what he could for Nathan. Then he would concentrate on mastering the secrets of the orb. He set off into the forest with Leah, listening intently as she recounted the conversation she had had with her father, detailing his suspicions of Bertrand Signac. She then proceeded to explain her plan.

"Father says we must search for evidence to clear him. But evidence will do us little good unless we can tie the murder to Cardinal Signac. Perhaps we can get a look at Arnaud de Gascon's body, to prove it was poison and not sorcery that killed him. For now, I have searched our house and found this. It isn't much, but it is a place to begin." Almost apologetically, Leah pulled a chunk of purplish wax from her apron. "Signac's men left this behind. It's a sample of the wax from which that cursed doll was formed."

Scorpio examined the wax. He looked at Leah questioningly.

"It's the color, you see. In the Jewish quarter we commonly use tallow—a wax made from animal fat. The color is a grayish white. Or we might use more costly beeswax candles. They are more sweetly scented, and are colored a tawny golden yellow. Sometimes the two are mixed together, or there may be herbs mixed into the tallow to improve the smell. But this wax has an unfamiliar texture and a strange, fruity odor, and it has been colored with some dyestuff I don't recognize. It is not used in the quarter, and is certainly not from our house. So I suggest we try to trace it. Let's go first to the marketplace. The merchants there supply the townspeople, including the courtiers and all their households. We shall pay a visit to the waxmaker's stall.''

The road was crowded with marketgoers, and the Pont d'Avignon even more so. Leah cautioned Scorpio to follow behind her at a discreet distance—it wouldn't do for a Jewish girl to be noted traveling in the company of a monk—and to keep his cowl well over his face. Cardinal Signac's men were still prowling the city on the lookout for Nathan's assistant, the escaped ''leper.''

''There may be some danger to you once we are at market,'' Leah added. ''There, as on the bridge, everyone observes everyone else. If you are noticed, you must flee from the marketplace to my grandmother's house, and she will hide you well. You will be safe among my people.''

Scorpio nodded obediently and trailed Leah into a dense maze of streets and alleys, many of them paved with cobbles or brick, all of them lined with busy shops and open stalls, makeshift booths and moving carts. Marketers haggled with vendors over wares of every description: meats and salt, butter and cheeses, honey, oil and spices, cloths and dyes, hatchets and knives, wines and beers. There were goldsmiths and blacksmiths, ironmongers and fishmongers, cobblers and saddlers, drapers, an armorer, and a wandering singer with a dancing bear on a leash. Hawkers shouted the prices of eels, of milk, of coal and bundles of faggots, of baskets, wineskins, crockery, cauldrons, of combs and needles and scents. Wheels squeaked, buyers bargained, children darted among the stalls, whetstones whirred, cleavers chopped, and pigs and fowl squealed at the butcheries.

Scorpio was overwhelmed. His mind was telling him to *Flee!* But where was the danger? He didn't see any of the cardinal's guards. *Flee* the noise and chaos, he assumed; it must be an instinctive agoraphobia that he'd never experienced before. It took all of his powers of concentration to override the unexpected panic and keep Leah in sight. So he did not notice the pair of flickering lights that tailed him, hanging behind and just above his head, weaving even as he did among the crowd.

Nor did Leah notice the lights in the air, so ubiquitous were the sparkling scissors and flashing scythes that were strung across the shopfronts, and the glinting signs and banners that

swung above the stalls. At intervals, briefly, she would glance
behind her to pick out the bobbing Benedictine hood from the
crowd at her heels. Occasionally she would pause to finger a
bolt of cloth or sniff at a jar of dried lavender, waiting for
Scorpio to catch up.

At length she stopped at a chandler's stall. It was situated
at a narrow crossroads, in an area of specialty shops that were
stocked with costly goods and patronized by the attendants of
the nobility. Well-dressed ladies with shopping baskets on their
arms sniffed at the perfumery and bargained for trinkets, while
skinny youths in the liveries of the finest houses juggled more
bulky parcels and straggled homeward with the most burden-
some purchases.

The chandler occupied a well-positioned corner stall. He had
open counters on two sides, and the whole was canopied in
bright, striped cloth. Behind the counters, vats of animal fat
and melted wax bubbled on low wood fires. Rows of finished
candles were arrayed on the counters, long and short, scented
and plain, twisted and straight. There were bundles of tapers
hanging from a rafter, and a fringe of long wicks made of
various fibers, and ceramic pots holding oils for lamps.

In a neighboring stall, a metalsmith sold ornate candlesticks
and candelabram, mortars and kettles, engraved vases and oil
lamps. How pretty they are, Leah thought, fingering the simple
lamp she still carried in her pocket from the previous night.

Craning her neck, she searched the crowd for Scorpio.
Across from the chandler, a breeder of hunting dogs exhibited
his wares for all to inspect. The elegant animals were chained
in a row to a horizontal beam, each collared in studded leather,
each with its own piggin of water. Opposite the houndsman,
on a diagonal from the chandler, was a falconer's stall, open
at the front and back but canopied and curtained on two sides.
The birds displayed were hooded and still but for one huge
raptor, chained at the ankle, who tore at a reddened piece of
meat.

Leah caught sight of the bobbing cowl. Scorpio had reached
the back of the falconer's stall, where the falconer tethered his
horse. The horse whinnied as Scorpio passed by, shuffling and
flaring his nostrils. Leah waited until she was sure Scorpio had
seen her, then turned to the chandler with her question.

The waxmaker was a cheerful fellow with a large square

face, flushed almost maroon from tending his cauldrons of boiling oil and wax. "My wife is usually here to help," he explained to Leah, giving one of the vats a vigorous stir, "but today she does her own marketing! Now, how can I help you?"

"What can you tell me about this kind of wax?" she asked as Scorpio joined her, his hood pulled well over his face.

The waxmaker turned the chunk of purplish wax over in his palm, smiling with recognition. "You didn't buy this from me, did you?" he asked. "It's rather exotic, you see. And as far as I know, I'm the only person in these parts to make it. It's a special mixture of beeswax with a bit of tallow for body, and my secret ingredient—a sort of mulberry. Gives it the color, you see. Different texture and scent, too. It's very expensive. Does the cardinal want more of it so soon?"

"The cardinal?" asked Leah, nudging Scorpio. She blinked and rubbed her eyes. She must be tiring, for she was starting to see little dots of light when she turned her head quickly. But she was too excited by the waxmaker's words to pay much attention to anything else. As it was, she had to strain to hear him above the din of the barking dogs. What could have set them off so? One would think there was a bear running loose through the marketplace!

"Cardinal Signac, of course," the waxmaker was saying. "Are you newly in his employ? I stock this wax for his household alone, for he prefers the color to any other, and claims that the scent reminds him of his boyhood. Didn't you come to market with his young butler and the guard over there?"

Leah looked behind her and turned away again with a jolt. Three of the cardinal's men were patrolling the marketplace. And they were accompanied by a young man in the cardinal's livery—the "messenger" who had been nervously waiting for Nathan's return on the morning of de Gascon's death!

Leah quickly concealed her face in the hood of her own cloak. "Scorpio!" she whispered. "Keep your face hidden and walk away from me, for the cardinal's men are about!" Was it her eyes? No! What were those lights flickering near his head? Her alarm doubled. "And look out for the little lights!" she urged, waving them away from Scorpio's face. Her hand seemed to pass right through them!

Scorpio dodged and ducked, batting at the lights as though they were biting flies, slapping at the air, trapping his sleeves in the long strands of wick that hung from the chandler's stall.

"Careful, there, Brother!" called the waxmaker as Scorpio tangled his tidy rows of wicks.

Scorpio tried to drag the clinging wicks from his sleeves as the lights spiraled closer. Catching his peaked hood in a row of hanging tapers, he struggled to pull free and whipped sharply toward the marketplace, yanking the disguising cowl from his head.

The waxmaker gasped as Scorpio's face was revealed.

Leah bent to help her friend, pulling at his hood and hitting away the whirling lights. But their intensity only seemed to grow.

"What *are* they?" she cried.

Attracted by the disturbance, the cardinal's men turned their attention to the waxmaker's stall.

"It's the leper!" shouted the captain of the guards.

"He's buying more wax! To murder another!" yelled the youthful butler. "Grab him!"

The cardinal's men strode purposefully to the waxmaker's stall, their weapons drawn, as Scorpio struggled to his feet. The lights dimmed and hung unmoving, one on either side of his head.

"Ho, there, sir!" the waxmaker cheerfully greeted the cardinal's young butler. He never liked to miss the opportunity of a sale. "More of the cardinal's special wax for you today?"

His words were cut short by a singing hum in midair, followed by a sickening thud. The waxmaker pitched forward, gurgling with blood, an arrow from a tiny assassin's crossbow neatly embedded in his throat.

Leah felt a scream rising in her lungs. "*Run!*" commanded Scorpio, shoving her out of the way. Grasping her sample of wax, Leah stumbled across the alley to the falconer's stall as the cardinal's men advanced on Scorpio.

"Take him!" commanded the captain of the guard.

The butler, satisfied, tucked his little crossbow back beneath his vest.

Leah watched in horror as a crowd gathered around the waxmaker's stall. Several of them moved to restrain the waxmaker's wife, just returned from her shopping, who wailed in anguish at the sight of her slain husband.

"This leper has murdered the waxmaker!" announced Signac's butler.

"Kill him!" came the response from the crowd.

One of the guards raised his sword, then lowered it, its tip poised at Scorpio's throat, to await the order from his captain.

The crowd, as one, sucked in its breath. Every eye sparkled with anticipation.

Soundlessly, in two explosive flashes of light, two red devils materialized from thin air, flanking Scorpio.

The crowd, as one, shrieked in terror.

"It's the devils! The leper commands the devils!" Some ran, some were frozen to the spot in horror and curiosity. Those who remained crossed themselves and clutched their neighbors, murmured prayers and peeked at the scene through squinted eyes. The waxmaker's wife screamed and tried to throw herself at their feet, begging for the soul of her husband.

Scorpio understood that the Hunters had found him at last. He didn't recognize the thin one. The other, strong and deadly, was Ardon the Stalker.

The devils frowned and pointed at the cardinal's men, swiftly, one by one. A spattering of thin, white beams of light sliced through the air, and the cardinal's men slumped to the ground, their mouths open in surprise, their eyes boggling and dead. There was a chorus of gasps from the terrified crowd.

Scorpio recognized the Hunters' weapons, delicate daggers that spit out white-hot beams of light. They were secured, like decorative spikes, at the bearers' wrists; so it was that it appeared to the assembled crowd as if the guards were felled by a mere devil's gesture, collapsing with steaming holes in their foreheads.

Stunned and fearful, the crowd backed away.

The Hunters grasped Scorpio between them, leveling their weapons at his chest, and hissed, one into each ear: "Where is the *orb*?"

Unable to let the matter rest, the breeder of hunting dogs, once the waxmaker's closest friend, shouted angrily from the safety of his stall. "The leper has summoned devils to do his dirty work! Witch! *Kill him!*'' Setting loose his dozen well-trained dogs, he stood back to watch the results of his life's work.

Barking and yowling with no thought of light beams or devils, the first pair of dogs attacked, leaping onto the two scarlet-skinned black-robed Hunters and sinking their teeth where they landed.

Again, death beams skewered the air and the two dogs fell howling, only to be replaced by their slavering kin.

Scorpio, momentarily ignored in the melee of gnashing teeth and laserfire, slipped through the tangle and left his captors to their fate. He slithered over the counter into the waxmaker's stall, unnoticed by the maddened crowd, who reveled in the fight and shouted with bloodlust like drunken peasants at a bear-baiting.

Scorpio made a sorrowful gesture of respect to the wax-maker's corpse. Then he slid through the side entrance of the stall, free to disappear into the streets of the marketplace. Where was Leah?

''There he is! After him!'' Scorpio recognized Ardon's voice. Looking across the open corner of the waxmaker's stall, he could see the two Hunters, still held in their tracks by a handful of dogs. Four beams of white light shot past him as he ducked across the alley. In the waxmaker's stall, the laserfire split a vat of boiling oil, which spilled onto the wood fire burning below. Instantly, with a wavelike roar, the shop burst into a wall of flames, fueled by oils and animal fats. The wooden counters caught first, then the hanging wicks and ta-pers; finally the body of the waxmaker was buried as the canopy of the fabric roof collapsed in a sheet of blazing stripes.

Panic swept through the crowd. Devils be damned—a fire could destroy the entire marketplace. ''He's set the stall on fire!'' screamed the falconer. ''Water!'' was the cry.

Already roused to activity, the houndsman gathered up his piggins of water by the armload and heaved them on the flaming stall, splashing the devils in the bargain. The devils shrieked and flapped their wet robes as their skins took on blotches of crimson.

From every direction, merchants and townspeople came running with buckets of water to douse the flames. The dripping

Hunters howled like ferocious infants. With the discovery that the same water that would quench an earthly conflagration could immobilize the devils with the pains of hellfire, the townspeople soon were pouring more liquid on their former tormentors than on the burning chandler's stall, satisfied to sacrifice more of their marketplace in order to gloat as the Hunters turned a fiery fuchsia.

Scorpio felt someone grab him from behind. "Stop struggling, it's me, Leah!" Leah scowled at him as though he had been very stupid.

"Why are you still here, so close to the flames?" She was struggling to control a frightened horse. "I'll stay to watch those devils. You must get out of here! I've unleashed the falconer's horse—now ride him to safety! My grandmother will hide you!"

With no further urging, Scorpio mounted the falconer's horse, who chose a direct route away from the marketplace and galloped as far from the fire as it could go.

Leah returned to her post behind the falconer's stall to watch the aftermath of her plan go up in flames. The devils were still howling for Scorpio, and screaming with pain as people drenched them with water. The waxmaker was dead and could no longer testify to help her father, and now Scorpio was accused of murder as well! The fire was almost under control, and the Pope's own soldiers, wearing shiny breastplates emblazoned with the six red roses of Clement's arms, had arrived to clear the market.

"It's the devils the Pope described!" shouted one of the soldiers, staring in wonder at the infernal scene.

The Hunters struggled to their feet. They were surrounded by some thirty men in primitive metal armor. Scorpio had escaped.

"You're under arrest," said the leader of the soldiers, nervously eyeing the pile of dogs and cardinal's guards lying at the devils' feet. The crowd was silent, and a smell of singed flesh and burning fur mixed with the oily smoke from the chandler's stall.

The Hunters looked wearily at one another and nodded.

There was no sense killing unnecessarily. Their skin was the color of red grapes and beginning to blister.

Lethor removed a glowing amber ball from the depths of his robe. He and Ardon grasped it between them. They held it lightly, in cupped hands, with arched fingers. Locking eyes, they nodded slightly and vanished.

In their wake, an astonished and hysterical crowd picked its way through the smoldering marketplace.

Leah, stunned and discouraged, slowly made her way back to the Jewish quarter, unnoticed and unremarked upon. But she nurtured a small joy: for she now recognized the devils as the Hunters Scorpio had described; she had seen another orb; and she had observed how they had used it.

Chapter
13

Grandmère Zarah shook her head grimly as she daubed at the smears of soot on Leah's cheeks and brushed the ashes from her hair. The milky gray cloud that obscured her vision seemed to grow denser day by day. Still, peering at her granddaughter's shadowy face, she could tell that the dark circles beneath Leah's reddened eyes would not wash away.

"You've had quite a time of it, my girl," she remarked. "You smell like a smokehouse."

Leah coughed, and grunted in shame. How would she explain to her grandmother that she had nothing more to show for all her trouble but the same lump of wax she had left home with the day before? Nathan was still in prison, and Scorpio was missing.

Zarah finished her ministrations and gave Leah a reassuring hug. "Never you mind. The healer is safe."

"So you have seen him!" Leah perked up at the news. "But what of the guards?" Zarah shrugged. Leah could see that the cardinal's men had already come and gone, searching for Scorpio. They had done their usual damage. In the kitchen alone, the wooden benches were overtuned, a heavy cupboard had been moved away from the wall, a barrel of grain emptied onto the floor.

"It's good that you are a girl," Zarah stated flatly. "No one thought to ask after you." Then her mood lightened, and she gave a wicked little laugh. "But young Mossé led those ruffians a merry chase on the falconer's horse! Scorpio was already hidden away by the time Signac's men arrived. While they were here making a mess of things, Mossé put on Scorpio's habit and galloped past our door as boldly as you please! One monk looks so much like another—you should have seen the cardinal's men run!''

Leah laughed. Then she lifted her eyebrows questioningly.

''The rabbi has hidden him in the cellar of the temple, where he can rest.'' Zarah was firm. ''Now you will rest as well. And then you will have a bath. Later you can join Scorpio if you wish. He has already told us of the fate of the waxmaker.''

Leah felt too full of sorrow to speak.

''It was not of your doing, granddaughter, you were not to blame. And do not lose hope. There is much we can do to help your father. Tonight, after dark, we will meet in the bread bakery. You had said that your father wished you and Scorpio to examine the body of Cardinal de Gascon. So, while you were off burning down the marketplace—''

Leah looked up sharply, ready to protest. But she could see that her grandmother was smiling gently, perhaps even with pride.

''—the rabbi and I have been hatching a plot of our own.''

Her grandmother's plan was clever. Leah smiled as her head touched the pillow. She slept deeply and woke with a start. She had dreamt that her father was calling her name. It was late afternoon, already dusk, too late to visit him today. But soon, she promised herself, she would bring him the news that he longed to hear, that she and Scorpio had found a way to set him free.

Rising quickly, Leah made her way to the women's bath-house in the public square. She left her clothing with an attendant in an anteroom, and hurried barefoot across the cold stone floor of the steamy bath chamber. Studiously ignoring the curious stares of the other women in the large wooden tub, she lowered herself into the hot, soothing water and closed her eyes. The women around her drew away as though she bore a communicable curse, and whispered among themselves.

Leah knew she was an object of gossip, that they longed to question her about the cardinal's murder, about her father's mysterious assistant, about the fire in the marketplace. Since the first day she had left the quarter to assist her father, the

.other women had treated her with a mixture of disapproval and envy. But something in her tired expression must have moved them to tact, for they were solicitous rather than malicious, and let her be.

At first, Leah was grateful to be left alone, excused from their questioning. If the truth be told, she had always encouraged the other women to see her as somehow apart from them, as a girl with aspirations. Different. Perhaps even better, she admitted, suddenly ashamed. For as she sat naked in the bath, one woman among others, she experienced a feeling of profound isolation. How comfortable these women were with one another, she thought wistfully, listening to their easy chatter and sympathetic laughter.

No one asked her anything. She had rejected their society and they had respected her choice. Some had shunned her, others were polite. But she was lost to them, and they to her. Leah had always assumed they were jealous of her learning and her small freedoms. Today in her loneliness, she was surprised to recognize in their expressions only pity, frank and resigned.

Leah understood that these same women offered unwavering sympathy to Grandmère Zarah. They wove themselves together as a safety net, stretched across the great pit of despair into which each of them might otherwise fall. Just as each of them had in her turn, they saw that Zarah had suffered a hard life; she had lost a husband and then a daughter-in-law; she had no grandsons, and the granddaughter was a problem, not yet married, such a disappointment; and now the tragedy with the doctor. . . . The women would visit Zarah, shoulder some of her grief, add their strength to hers, gather round. For the first time Leah understood her grandmother's pain on her behalf. She understood that the women pitied her for losing her way. For losing them.

But self-pity was an unproductive luxury, and Leah would not allow herself to wallow. Not today. Not as long as her father was a prisoner.

It was growing dark when Leah let herself into the synagogue. The square stone building, the hub of all community activity, was curiously quiet tonight, its special meeting rooms deserted. There were no groups of boys reciting their lessons, no gossipers or storytellers, no family gatherings or wedding preparations. It was as though by some mysterious signal the Jews of Avignon had agreed to avoid the temple, while the rabbi and the councilors of the quarter met among themselves. Only in the temple proper were there voices to be heard: Rabbi de Lunel conducting an evening service, joined by the singsong cant of the other men.

Leah made her way directly to the dark stone staircase leading to the cellar, hoping to have some time alone with Scorpio before the rabbi and the others arrived. Scorpio was something she had that was special, she thought. Something apart.

She pushed open a heavy wooden door and breathed deeply. Leah had always loved the low, vaulted chambers beneath the temple, with their mixed odors of stone and mortar, smoky oil from the flickering lamps, cold spring water and baking bread. For here were the great community bread ovens, where Jewish bakers fashioned the round or braided *challot* loaves for the Sabbath, and baked the flat, unleavened *matzoh* bread for the eight days of Passover. Families who had a feast to prepare, or those too poor to have ovens of their own, came to the synagogue to cook their meals. In yet another subterranean hall was the deep stone tub where the pious carried their dead to be cleansed. And beneath it all, down another long flight of steps, was the underground pool of the *mikvah*, the ritual bath, cool and dark, that rose and fell with the swelling of the moon, fed, as it was, by the sparkling waters of the Fountain of Vaucluse.

Torches had been lit along a narrow corridor that led toward the farthest reaches of the cellar, where the bread ovens were built into the thick stone walls. Leah peered into every chamber along the way, searching for the unlikely figure of a Benedictine monk in a Jewish synagogue. There was a sound of dripping water, and she followed it.

Scorpio lay naked, faceup, in the coffin-shaped stone tub reserved for the dead. His eyes were closed and his waterlogged skin had turned a chalky gray. He lay in the water with his arms floating at his sides, his tiny nostrils and bony knees just breaking the surface. A trickle of water dripped rhythmically from a stone spout at his feet, sending a shallow spiral of ripples along each thigh. Near his head, folded neatly as a pillow, was a white shroud.

They've drowned him, Leah thought dully. She let out an anguished groan and fell to her knees at the edge of the tub. Her eyes welled with tears, but she made no other sound. For some minutes she wept in silence with her head bowed. Please don't let this be happening, she prayed. She could not bear to look at him. She wanted to protect him. He was her friend, she realized with the first flush of grief. He was her friend, and still she found his appearance grotesque. She would have to pull him from the tub and dress him, then wait for the others to come.

Leah lifted her chin and prepared to undertake the job at hand.

Scorpio rose from the tub with no help from Leah, water cascading from his skin in sheets, and opened his eyes.

Screaming in abject terror, Leah backed away from the rising demon. He hadn't been breathing, she could swear it. Now he lived. His face showed fright almost equal to hers, changing to almost obsequious concern. She watched, frozen, as Scorpio, with excruciating politeness, lifted the shroud and slipped it over his head. The garment, she could see, was nothing more than a white baker's smock, two sizes too big for him, dusty with flour and dotted with bits of dough.

"I-I thought you were dead," she managed to croak, still trembling. "Th-this is where we wash our dead."

Scorpio's eyes seemed to widen, and he lifted a hand to his mouth. Then he made the peculiar warbly sound that Leah recognized as laughter.

Leah's temper flared. "What a fright you've given me! How could you just float there like that?" she scolded, even as she was flooded with relief. Scorpio's skin, as white as his apron, began to glow like pearls.

Scorpio swallowed his mirthful trilling. "I am sorry," he said contritely. "I needed water, and I was sleeping."

"I have *news*," Leah continued impatiently. "After you fled, the townspeople practically boiled your Hunter friends with buckets of water. And then the Pope's men arrived and tried to arrest them!"

Scorpio let out a peal of gargles.

"They were very angry that you'd gotten away!"

Scorpio knew he should be worried, but the thought of the Hunters thus foiled filled him with heady delight. This peculiar planet seemed to inspire him to extremes of emotion. He must try harder to keep himself in check!

"They had another *orb*!" Leah insisted. "I saw them use it!"

"You saw how it worked?" Scorpio sobered at once.

"I'll show you," said Leah. "In the bakery. We'll wait for the others." Scorpio skipped eagerly ahead of her, his baker's smock flapping around his skinny ankles. She would never have imagined that a demon could be so silly. With a deep sign of cheerful hope and fond exasperation, Leah followed him to the basement chamber that served as a bakery for the thousand Jews of the quarter.

The cavelike room was still warm from the day's baking. Indeed, with its low, barrel-vaulted ceiling and arched walls of grainy stone and brick, all bleached white with a dusting of flour, the room both looked and smelled like the inside of a loaf of bread. On two sides of the room, thick stone slabs served as worktables. The larger of the tables, made of a dark, slate-colored stone, was built against an outer wall of the synagogue. At the back of the table was a polished wooden post pinned to an iron swivel, a permanent rolling pin that stretched diagonally to the ceiling, where it rested in a great iron hook like the mast of some stranded ship. At the very top of the wall, night air filtered through a grilled window that opened to a cobbled courtyard behind the temple.

Climbing onto the table, Leah stood on tiptoe and peered through the iron bars into the night. The courtyard was deserted. Scorpio pulled a wooden bench to the center of the chamber as she clambered down again.

"They held the orb between them, like this," Leah whispered, seating herself. She cupped her hands, arching her fingers so that the tips defined the shape of a small sphere. Then she dropped her hands and shrugged. "That's all. They stared at one another and nodded, and then they vanished."

Scorpio looked puzzled. "It doesn't sound very mysterious, does it? But I will try it. Perhaps there are pressure points on the orb I hadn't noticed before."

"They killed a lot of people," Leah said reproachfully. "And they would have killed you. How did they find you, these Hunters of yours?"

"I don't know. But I will have to move quickly, before they

find me again, and before I become the cause of more deaths. They want only me. But they care for no one.''

Leah had no doubt that Scorpio—demon, angel, or whatever he might be—was in the gravest of trouble. She had witnessed the ferocity of the Hunters, and had felt for herself the power that emanated from the ball of light. "Scorpio, you must not be seen in Avignon," she began slowly. "You are hunted by the marshal for the murder of the waxmaker, and for setting fire to the marketplace. The cardinal's men are after you, and the Pope's men too.''

"I must leave this place.''

"I know. I will find a way to fetch your orb. In return, I am hoping you will agree to the plan my grandmother and the rabbi have conceived to help my father.''

"And a good plan it is, too!'' Mossé de Milhans, the man Grandmère Zarah affectionately called "young Mossé," strode into the bakery. He was a strapping man of thirty, a successful textile merchant admired for his forthright manner, a quality that was enhanced tenfold by his cheerful temperament. A widower of two years, he had also lost three of his four children to the Black Death. But he was known to rejoice that he had been spared to care for his only son. And it was very well known that Mossé de Milhans was in search of a new wife.

"Hello, Leah.'' Mossé's greeting was warm, and his smile was genuine. Leah smiled back, but her greeting was formal. She liked Mossé very much—who wouldn't?—but she knew that Zarah had been practicing her matchmaking skills, and she feared Mossé was responding. He would make a perfect husband, Leah admitted. He was hardworking, kind and devout. But it was out of the question. He would soon have her mothering a houseful of children, and, while he might be proud of her learning, he would never allow her to continue. And what did he know of the world, of poetry and courtly manners?

Leah caught herself and turned away, blushing. She had been staring speculatively at Mossé de Milhans, and he had gazed back, a puppyish look in his eyes.

"Here is a present, Scorpio the Healer.'' Mossé broke the awkward silence, tossing a bundle to Scorpio. Scorpio unrolled a crisp new monk's habit and slipped it over his head, pulling the cowl as far forward as it would go.

Mossé waited respectfully. He supposed the Healer must be

accustomed to the shadowy hood; no doubt he had suffered countless taunts and persecutions. The disfigurement was horrible, even he had to admit. Perhaps the Lord had burdened him in proportion to his gifts. Young Leah was certainly showing her backbone, working with such a frightening figure to save the good doctor. She had strength and beauty both.

Rabbi de Lunel arrived, escorting Grandmère Zarah on one arm. He was followed by a thin man in his twenties who carried a bag of carpenter's tools on his shoulder and a short wooden bench under his arm. Leah rose to sit with her grandmother, and the four men occupied the longer bench.

"So, Mossé," began the rabbi, "you must tell us of your adventure with the falconer's horse."

Mossé beamed delightedly. "The guards chased me through the streets of the quarter, out of the gate in rue des Marchands and almost to the river. Then I led them right back into the marketplace. Such a maze! 'Now we'll have him!' shouted the guards. But never has a monk ridden so wildly! The market had been cleared of buyers for the day, and was still smoldering. I galloped through the streets until I could see the guards were ready to trap me—they split into two groups and set out to head me off. Before they could get ahead of me, I took a corner sharply, so I was out of their sight. Then I hopped from the falconer's horse, doffed the habit, draped it over the poor steed and spurred him on his way. Then I hid in an empty shop. Half of the guards pursued the riderless horse, who trotted home to the falconer's stall, for there I saw him, munching on smoky hay, as I made my way home."

"But didn't they search the shops for Scorpio?" asked Leah. "And didn't they find the Benedictine habit?"

"You are quite right to ask," Mossé said admiringly. My, the girl was intelligent.

Leah winced as Zarah's elbow nudged her ribs.

"The guards searched the shops," Mossé went on. "They found me right away—for I ran from the shop and summoned them myself. 'The leper!' I cried. 'I saw him ride past my shop on a horse, and then he seemed to disappear into thin air!' We all ran together to the falconer's stall, and there stood the horse, with Scorpio's old habit draped over its back. Naturally they searched. High and low. But they found no sign of a naked leper." Mossé looked at Scorpio apologetically, but the Healer seemed to take no offense, so he continued. "'He's disappeared, all right,' said one of the guards. 'Those devils must have come for him,' said another. So the guards took the habit back to the cardinal, as evidence that the culprit had simply vanished!"

At this everyone in the room roared with laughter.

"You are brilliant, Mossé," said Zarah, her elbow busy at work again.

"The Christians have gone devil-crazy," said the rabbi, shaking his head in wonder.

"Everyone is having visions of red devils and the fires of Hell," said the carpenter. "They talk of nothing else."

"They may be ridiculous, but they are dangerous," said the rabbi. The group nodded soberly.

Scorpio felt strangely, sadly, at home among this small group of earthbeings. He was reminded of the secret resistance meetings that had taken place on Terrapin, gatherings of the hurt and frightened, who faced their oppressors as did this group, with courage, hope and humor. They had thought of themselves as a gathering of gnats, insignificant one at a time, effective as a missile in a swarm. But the Hunters had killed the Speakers among them, one by one, and the swarm had never congealed into a missile, or even into a pellet. Who is left to defend the Aquay? Scorpio wondered bitterly. Now there may be just me. Scorpio the tenacious gnat.

". . . the habit?" Leah was saying. "Didn't you bring Scorpio a new habit?"

"I am a textile merchant, am I not?" said Mossé, his eyes twinkling. Again, the group laughed.

"We must hasten to business," said Grandmère Zarah. The gathering fell respectfully quiet. "Rabbi de Lunel and I have devised a way to smuggle Scorpio into the Cathedral of Notre-Dame-des-Doms, where they have taken Cardinal de Gascon's body. No one here can doubt the innocence of my son Nathan in this ghastly death. But before we take action to accuse another, my son wishes us all to be certain in our own hearts that the cardinal's death was caused by poison—a dose of poison administered by one of his own kind. Because it is Nathan's wish that Leah also inspect the corpse, she will go as well. And I pray, Rabbi, that it will be with your blessing."

Rabbi de Lunel rose to speak. "It was Zarah who brought

to my attention some of the assets of our community that we tend to overlook. It is well known, for example, that Jews are forbidden to join the trade guilds, or to practice crafts that the Christians wish to keep for themselves. But it is also known that in practice, Jews are permitted to patronize their own tradesmen within these walls, and that some of our most talented tradesmen are frequently commissioned to do specialty work for Christian clients—as long as the transaction is arranged through a Christian guild member.''

"And as long as the lion's share of the profit goes to the Christian guild member!'' added the carpenter.

The rabbi laughed ruefully. "Salomon, here, our most renowned cabinetmaker, recently received a shipment of wood from his cousin, a timber merchant. It is the finest mahogany to be found in all of Avignon, sent here from distant North Africa. And Salomon, as Zarah pointed out to me, had just ordered a quantity of plush crimson satin, cloth of the heaviest weight, from our friend Mossé. We put two and two together. And so we have brought Salomon here tonight to ask him if perhaps he has received an interesting commission from the Christian Carpenter's Guild.''

"Indeed I have,'' said Salomon, his eyes twinkling merrily. "For there is no one else in all of Avignon who could build a box as fancy as mine.'' Beckoning to Scorpio, he pulled a set of measuring sticks from his carpenter's bag. "But what is *most* interesting is the fact that I received the commission *before* our last Sabbath—the day *before* the banquet at the palace. *Two* days before Arnaud de Gascon died!''

"To ensure the effectiveness of Zarah's ruse, we must gather every bit of evidence we can,'' Rabbi de Lunel added. "Leah has already uncovered the truth about the wax. She and Scorpio will identify the poison that was used. And Salomon will try to discover who placed the telltale order with the Carpenter's Guild.''

"Excuse me,'' Scorpio ventured. "But why I am being measured, I don't understand. What did the messenger order from Salomon?''

"Forgive me for my bad manners, Master Scorpio, I thought you knew,'' said the rabbi. "Scorpio the Healer, allow me to present to you—Salomon the Coffinmaker!''

Chapter
14

The coffin was a work of art, superbly crafted and elegantly shaped. The dark grain of the African mahogany had been rubbed and polished to bring out its plum-colored highlights. Inside, a sleek satin lining of the brightest cherry red, lightly cushioned and embroidered in golden threads with the crest of the de Gascons, perfectly complemented the glossy wood. On either end, the gilded handles were decorated with finials in the shapes of the winged evangelists, a lion, an eagle, an ox and a man. Each of the figures had jeweled eyes, subtle points of bloodred ruby. It was just as Salomon had said, Leah thought, running her hand along the smooth contour of the gently swelling lid: no one could have made a better box.

She tugged uncomfortably at the vest she wore over an unfamiliar tunic and breeches, and checked that her hair was hidden beneath the workman's cowl that framed her face. Straining anxiously, she tried to catch a last glimpse of her reflection in the coffin's sheen as Salomon and Mossé tossed a simple tarpaulin over the weighty container and tied it to the two-wheeled handcart on which it lay.

"You look fine, Leah," said Mossé reassuringly. "No one would ever suspect you are not a boy." Not unless they notice the rather too-large eyes, he thought, the full lips and soft cheeks. . . . Mossé quickly checked his impure thoughts. Flushing deeply, he kicked at the wooden wedges that held the cart wheels immobile, and threw his weight against its two long handles. Salomon steadied his masterpiece from the back, then shifted to take his side of the handcart as it began to roll.

· "You will walk behind us, Leah," Salomon directed. He grunted as he and Mossé pulled the handcart between them. "You are my new apprentice, and your name is—what *is* your name for the day?"

Leah bit her lip and tried to choose a boy's name for herself. She followed the two men out of the shop and into the narrow lanes of the quarter, observing how they struggled when their way was rutted or rough.

"I am your apprentice, correct?" she said finally. "So you would just call me 'boy.' And I should help you push." Bracing herself against the back of the cart, she added her weight to the undertaking.

Mossé and Salomon exchanged a look of dismay.

"Leave it to us, boy!"

Leah heard an angry, warning edge to Mossé's command. It wouldn't do for her to take her disguise too seriously, he seemed to say. The men were putting themselves in great danger to help her and her father, and they were already pushed to their limits. Wisely, she backed off and walked behind the cart in as servile a manner as she could muster.

"That's better." Mossé was appeased.

In the streets closest to the palace, the cart rolled more smoothly. But as they approached the Cathedral of Notre-Dame-des-Doms, the two men seemed to bristle with tension.

"Here comes the Christian carpenter who will act as broker," Salomon whispered to Leah. "His name is Séguret. He is a high-ranking member of the Carpenter's Guild. Don't worry, he'll have little interest in a lowly apprentice."

Leah hoped that Salomon was right. The man striding toward them looked like a successful tradesman, but the fringe of fur that trimmed his goatskin hat bespoke a conceit not quite fitting to his station.

-"You're late," began M. Séguret. Salomon tightened his grip on the cart.

"I see you've brought my casket," Séguret continued, as if to take possession not only of the object but of its creation as well.

Salomon was a patient man. But, although he was secure in the knowledge that his skill and talent were superior to the

cocky guild member's, it rankled that M. Séguret would make
more money for little more than an hour of his time than would
Salomon, who had labored tirelessly for a week to finish the
casket by the appointed hour. It rankled even more that Séguret
would take the credit as well. But for Nathan's sake, it was
important that all should go well.

"It's a terrible thing about Cardinal de Gascon," Salomon
remarked casually. "But how fortunate a coincidence that such
a casket as this was almost completed on the day he died. I
am honored to know that such an illustrious personage as he
will go to his rest in *my* handiwork."

Séguret took the bait at once, and glowered at Salomon. "It
was indeed fortunate, was it not, that Cardinal Signac had
commissioned *me* to supply him with a handsome casket of
the finest wood? The cardinal has been exceedingly generous,
in my opinion. Do you know that he had ordered this casket
for an elderly member of his own family, who, God be thanked,
still lives? But when Signac heard of the fate of his dear colleague, Arnaud de Gascon, he immediately donated this casket
to his memory. And of course we appreciate your contribution,
Salomon. After all, it's the least that *you* people can do, seeing
that it was one of your own who murdered de Gascon!"

"Why, you—" Leah caught herself and clamped her mouth
shut.

"Why, let's make haste to the sacristy, then," Mossé in-
terjected cheerfully, hauling with renewed vigor on the heavy
cart.

The Cathedral of Notre-Dame-des-Doms soared above the
city of Avignon from its favored site on the rocky precipice of
the Rocher des Doms. The building was insulated by the Palace
of the Popes on its southern flank, and the gardens and stables
of the Papal See on the bluff to the north.

Breathing hard with effort, Salomon and Mossé began the
climb to the cathedral. For the last stage of the journey up the
steep hill, they rested a moment, then changed positions. Mossé
applied his shoulder to the back of the cart and pushed, while,
under the watchful eye of M. Séguret, Leah took her logical
place next to Salomon at the front of the cart and pulled.

"Something of a weakling, that apprentice of yours," Séguret observed to Salomon as he strode authoritatively ahead, making no effort to help.

Salomon rolled his eyes at Leah, his lips curling with amusement. Then he heaved, guiding the cart toward the rear of the cathedral, where a small wooden door led directly to the sacristy. So far, all had gone well.

It was cold in the sacristy. Leah held the door ajar, shivering, as Salomon and Mossé unfastened the tarpaulin, slid the mahogany coffin from the cart and gently deposited it on a wide stone slab at the center of the floor. Although there was incense burning in all four corners, the vaulted chamber smelled of death.

Near the casket, on a stone bench along one wall, the cardinal's body had been laid out, ready to be prepared for burial. The corpse was covered with a cloth of white linen that was embroidered with an ornate cross and neatly tucked around the head and feet. On a table next to the remains were a robe and hat of cardinal's red, and the brocade vestments dotted with pearls, the sapphire ring and coral rosary, the jeweled cross and jewel-encrusted prayer book that de Gascon would bear as he lay in state, waiting to be laid to his eternal rest.

Leah shuddered and bowed her head, dreading the job that must follow.

"You are an artist indeed," M. Séguret said grudgingly, patting Salomon sharply on one shoulder. "The casket is as beautiful a one as I have ever seen." Despite himself, Salomon looked pleased. "If you two will come with me, we shall attend to the financial transaction," Séguret continued. "Your boy can wait outside with the cart."

Leah shot a panicked look at Mossé, who shrugged and followed the others back outside the sacristy. Leah had no choice but to join them as well.

The three men disappeared in the direction of the palace, and Leah was on her own. The door to the sacristy was guarded by an indifferent-looking monk who nodded as she settled down on the cart. She had to think of a way to get back inside, and quickly.

"It's a terrible tragedy, the cardinal dying so suddenly," she said in a gruff, low voice.

"We all must meet our Maker," the monk responded patly.

"If it would please you, Brother, I'd like to give the casket a final polishing. It's made of mahogany, come all the way from Africa!"

"You don't say? That's a kind offer, boy, especially coming from one of your kind. Come with me, then. I'd like to see this fine casket myself!"

Leah groaned inwardly. Now how would she get rid of him?

"They'll be coming to dress him soon, so you'll have to hurry." The monk led Leah down the short corridor that led to the sacristy. "And I'll have to get back outside. I'm supposed to be guarding the robes and jewels, you see."

Good, he would only stay for a moment. Leah removed a soft cloth from her vest and slowly began to polish the lid of the already radiant coffin. "I won't be long if you have to get back outside," she said.

But the monk seemed to be in no particular hurry. "So this is African mahogany," he said, circling the casket. "It's so shiny!" He ran a hand along the glossy wood. "Seems solid enough!" He knocked three times on the fitted lid. "What's it like inside?"

But Leah was pressing down on the lid in horror. Three knocks—that was the signal!

The lid thumped under her hands.

"What was that?" gasped the monk, pulling Leah away from the coffin. As they both stood back in horror, the lid of the coffin slowly raised, and an apparition stepped forth. It was a bright red figure in a white Benedictine robe.

The monk froze, a whimpering quaver rising in his throat. Then he bolted from the sacristy, screaming in terror. "A devil! Another devil, come to take the cardinal! And he's right in the cathedral!"

Leah, too, was horrified. Scorpio's face and hands had turned a flaming crimson.

"I've taken on color from the satin lining, you left me in there for so long," Scorpio said between deep breaths of open air. "Don't stare like that, we've got to hurry now!"

With trembling hands, Leah drew back the snowy cloth from Cardinal de Gascon's face. The sickening sweetish odor of decay was strong, and already the face had begun to blacken.

"I cannot look," she faltered, pulling away. She hadn't had

to look into the face of death since the Black Plague had swept
off northward, two years before. She wasn't sure she had the
courage to look again. "Please, will you examine his eyes,"
she asked Scorpio beseechingly. "The pupils should be fixed
and dilated. I'll check the fingernails for any seeds or bits of
foodstuff that might have lodged there." She felt along the
linen shroud, locating a stiff hand. A new wave of nausea
struck.

"Sit down next to the table," Scorpio directed firmly. "Just
tell me what to do. The pupils are greatly dilated. What does
that mean?"

"It's consistent with my father's diagnosis of aconite poisoning—but it could mean many other things as well. Is there
an odor of almonds about the mouth?"

Grimly determined, Scorpio opened the cardinal's mouth and
pushed down gently on his chest. A slight puff of foul-smelling
air escaped the purpling lips. But it told him nothing.

"Check the chest cavity," Leah whispered. "Quickly!"

Scorpio drew the sheet away from the body. "This man has
been embalmed," he said quietly, "and disemboweled. The
stomach cavity is stitched up and empty. We will find no
evidence here."

"Inside his mouth!" Leah urged. "The last thing!"

Holding his breath, Scorpio turned his face away and
searched with his fingers in the dead man's mouth. The teeth
had been neglected. Several were loose. One of them, a lower
rear molar, came away in his hand.

"We've got it," he said, fighting disgust, willing a feeling
of triumph to overtake him. Embedded in the rotten tooth was
a single black seed, like a poppy seed, but slightly larger.

Leah had recovered sufficiently to look. "Monkshood!" she
whispered. "Now there can be no doubt! But we'd better get
out of here before we're accused of defiling a corpse!"

Scorpio handed Leah the tooth and covered the cardinal,
tucking the linen neatly back in place.

Leah closed the lid of the coffin and watched while Scorpio
washed his hands in a font of carved stone. Then, as Scorpio's
color faded from pink to peach to the familiar Benedictine
white, she had an idea. Grabbing the cardinal's plain red hat
and robe, she concealed them under her tunic.

There were noises coming from the doorway that led into

the cathedral. "He's in here, I swear to you, he climbed right out of the coffin," the monk was babbling. He was answered by the sound of tromping feet and rattling swords.

Scorpio and Leah raced for the corridor and out the sacristy door, where Salomon and Mossé were anxiously waiting. Scorpio dove under the tarpaulin that lay in a heap on the cart, and the three Jewish carpenters trundled safely away.

Chapter
15

Would he be there? Aimeric could hardly be considered dependable, Leah thought as she slipped quietly through the darkened alleys of the quarter. It was the dinner hour. Here and there small windows glowed with golden light, broken by the shadowy movements of the families gathered within. Leah felt a pang of longing as sharp and debilitating as a sudden wound, a longing for a family dinner taken at hearthside. She pictured just such a dinner as those she used to find so dreary, with her grandmother humming, her father at prayer and herself staring into the firelight and dreaming of—freedom from such dinners.

Leah bit her lip and hurried through the darkness, wondering how many other ways she could find this night to prove herself a fool. She must have been mad to think Aimeric was interested enough in her welfare to help. But if he wasn't there to meet her, she had already decided she would go on to Villeneuve by herself. She was little concerned with her own safety, not with her father in such desperate straits. If anything should happen to her, Grandmère Zarah would be well taken care of by her friends in the quarter. And Scorpio was safely hidden in a chamber beneath the synagogue, in hope that the Hunters would have a harder time finding him if he stayed underground. If she was caught, Mossé could fetch the orb for him, wherever it was.

Leah had seen her father late in the afternoon. The change was alarming. He looked weak and sallow, and his garments had hung on him, rumpled and limp, as though he had suddenly shrunk. He had not been allowed to leave his cell, nor had it been cleaned. The odor was terrible. He had apologized for it, tried to disguise his shame, told her that one got more accustomed to it after a time. He said he had been eating and sleeping, and that he was hopeful all would be well. But his eyes were sunken, and there were bruises on his face and arms. Leah knew he was lying to spare her pain.

"I have encouraging news," she had said, describing the rare wax and the tiny seed from the monkshood plant she and Scorpio had discovered in de Gascon's tooth. "There can be no doubt that Signac was behind the poisoning." But the wax-maker had died in a fire in the marketplace, she had explained; and even if they admitted despoiling the corpse of a cardinal to obtain the tooth, they couldn't prove that the seed was embedded in the tooth when they found it. Still, it was something.

Leah had carefully avoided any mention of devils. How could she explain that Scorpio was pursued by scarlet beings who could kill with beams of light? Nor did she detail the plan she had concocted, for how could she tell her father that Scorpio could change his skin? She wasn't even sure what she thought of these things herself. For now, she was simply proceeding on faith.

But Nathan was filled with new hope. "Some of the guards seem to fear me," he remarked. "It seems all of Avignon is seeing devils. Even the Pope! But the visions are working to my advantage, for the uproar is so great that they've neglected to set a date for my tribunal in the Consistory. I guess I have the Devil himself to thank!" He had winked at Leah, and she had managed a weak smile.

"In truth, I thank God for the delay, and I believe he answers my prayers," he went on. His tone had grown serious, but not somber. "Now we have our proof! I couldn't have made that doll. You needn't show the authorities the tooth. We can tell them of the wax! You did well to find Scorpio, daughter. And the knowledge that your grandmother and the rabbi, and Salomon and Mossé, all of you have worked so cleverly on my behalf—it fills my heart with hope. Have you looked for the baker of the fatal 'poppy seed' cake? All that remains is to find a way to tie the poison firmly to Bertrand Signac."

Leah sighed. They would say that her father had conspired with the waxmaker, and that Scorpio had murdered the waxmaker to ensure his silence. That the baker was in Nathan's service. That Signac's order for a fancy casket was a happy coincidence. Their evidence proved nothing. But she kept silent. Nathan had confirmed what Leah had already planned to do next. She would pay a visit to the household of Bertrand Signac. She would have to go alone, for it was dangerous for Scorpio to risk being seen. And neither could she risk being seen, or her plan would be spoiled, so she would have to go by night.

"Keep us all in your prayers, Father," is all Leah had said. "For I think we have devised a way to assure that the true murderer is revealed. If we are successful, the Pope will hear the confession of Bertrand Signac himself!"

After dark, Leah knew, the Pont d'Avignon was the province of thieves and cutthroats, prostitutes and drunkards. For a young girl crossing alone, the danger would be great. Even if she dressed as a man, it was likely she would be accosted if she traveled on foot. Leah needed an escort. Someone with a horse. Someone at home in the night world of the bridge, who wouldn't much care that she thought it necessary to sneak into a mansion in Villeneuve-lès-Avignon. Someone with a few loose scruples, but who might feel inclined to do her a favor.

The solution was painfully obvious: Aimeric de la Val d'Ouvèze. She would have to swallow her pride and face him once again. Leah agonized over how she would convince him. Must she humble herself and beg? Embarrass him into a chivalrous position? Join him in his bed?

When finally she located him, browsing, she presumed, for the tastiest "fruits" in the fecund little square off the rue des Marchands, she decided on a direct appeal. Aimeric had looked up with satisfaction at her approach, as if he'd know all along that she must find him irresistible. But she thought that his greeting held a grain of honest pleasure as well.

"I need your help to get into Bertrand Signac's mansion," she had said. "Just a ride across the bridge, and perhaps a little distraction at the gate." Much to her surprise Aimeric de la Val d'Ouvèze had required no coaxing.

"Truly you *are* a sorceress, little Leah," he had answered.

"Though your plan is likely to fail, you know—for you are no match for the wiles of Bertrand Signac. But when I am with you, my judgement seems to melt like butter. You have such loyalty! Coupled with such passion! Of course I will help you. I am at your service, fair maiden, in this your time of travail."

In fact, Aimeric had been as surprised as Leah at the quickness with which he had acquiesced. But there was something about her he found compelling. Perhaps it was the way she had called him a coward at their last meeting; or maybe he was just a little sorry he had hurt her feelings, and sorry that her father would be executed, as surely as the sun sets. Her beauty moved him, and he liked her. He knew he shouldn't waste his time on a Jewess. But he especially liked her when she needed him. How could she be so naive as to think she could bargain with Bernard Signac? He'd just go along for protection—and besides, he was bored.

Leah realized with shocked amusement that Aimeric must think she intended to throw herself at the cardinal's mercy and plead for her father's release, perhaps sacrifice her virtue in exchange for a pardon. Or even that she intended to murder Bertrand Signac in his bed! Why would he risk an involvement in such a scheme? But Leah did not question Aimeric's motives. She was fortunate to have caught her former suitor in one of his more courtly moods. "I shall be ever in your debt," she had said graciously, not missing the twinkle of acquisitiveness that flashed across Aimeric's visage.

"You may have scorned my advances once; but it pleases me that you do not find me completely without advantages," Aimeric replied.

"I merely intend to search for a way to prove my father's innocence," Leah had ventured. "Or Signac's guilt."

Aimeric had shrugged noncommittally. "I have no love for Bertrand Signac. Besides, as posts are vacated at the top, more positions open at the bottom. Everyone advances when cardinals fall." So that was it! Leah wondered if her surprise showed. She had never thought of Aimeric as a man with ambition. Was he hoping for an appointment at court? "My uncle, the bishop, would then be in line for a cardinalship," he'd continued. Ah, that explained it: his ambition was not for himself, but for his guardian. "And if you are caught, they would never associate me with you," he'd added wryly.

Leah had disregarded that remark. In fact, she was grateful that it was true. Even such a rake as Aimeric would be unlikely to be gallivanting about the mansions of Villeneuve in the dead of night with a Jewess. But she had no wish to endanger him, and it was reassuring to know that, should anything go wrong, Aimeric would be protected by his noble birth. If it pained her to accept that Aimeric's motives were less than altruistic, she hid it well. She had gone on to explain the details of the night's foray. She needed to get into a downstairs chamber, and she needed to search the garden.

"You'll have to distract the dogs," Aimeric noted. "Signac is known for his stables and his kennels."

Leah had been pleased that Aimeric was showing an interest in her plan. But she was frightened as well. She wouldn't have thought of the dogs. There were bound to be other dangers she hadn't anticipated.

She must have looked stricken. "Don't worry," Aimeric had said at once. "I'll bring meat. This is beginning to sound like quite an adventure! Perhaps you will be so grateful to me that you'll—"

Aimeric had broken off. He had meant his remark to be taken lightly. But it seemed he was always putting his foot into his mouth with this strangely fetching girl. Would he never remember that she just didn't know how to flirt?

"Anything," Leah had muttered. "I'll repay you in any way I can. But not until my father walks free."

Aimeric had rolled his eyes. "I may have to wait forever, then."

Leah, stirred at last to anger by Aimeric's calm conviction of her father's doom, lifted her hand to slap his face. But, anticipating her fury, he had grabbed her hand in midair and pressed it to his lips, as though he had realized his tactlessness. "I will meet you tonight, then," he said with a flourish, "under circumstances I, for one, sincerely wish were other than they are!"

Then Leah had watched him stride off down the rue des Marchands, feeling as flustered as a schoolgirl.

Leah paid the guard at the gate in the rue Jacob, slipping him something extra to let her through. "I know it is after dark, but one of my father's patients—a lady who wishes to remain anonymous, you understand?—is having the pains of labor two months before her time. I have some tea for her, to ease her pain.''

The guard winked knowingly. This was gossip-ridden Avignon, after all, where an early birth meant the lady had been entertaining while her husband was away at war. So the doctor's daughter had a baby to deliver, what business was it of his? ''Discretion is everything, is it not, mademoiselle?''

Leah walked through the gate and into the night. In the deep shadow of a deserted alley, Aimeric waited impatiently, shifting from one foot to the other and twisting the leather reins of his horse into a sweaty knot. By the time Leah rushed up to meet him, she was slightly out of breath and flushed with excitement.

''Let's go!'' she whispered. Aimeric lifted her onto the horse, then mounted himself, so that she was sitting sidesaddle in front of him. His arms encircled her, and as he leaned forward to adjust the reins, he could smell the hair that was bound at her neck. He breathed deeply and tightened his hold as he kicked his brown mare and broke into a sudden, bounding canter toward the Pont d'Avignon.

Leah drew in a sharp breath and struggled to maintain her composure as she jounced against the padded saddle on the horse's broad back. Aimeric held her steadily against him, and she could feel his breath in her hair. She fastened her gaze on the route ahead and tried to concentrate on her plan for the night. But what could she do about the alarming warmth that was invading her limbs, bathing her skin like a hot salve? Something was stirring her, as though her body was a cauldron, as though her blood was slowly boiling on the hearth.

So this was what it was like. The heat rises, the will dissolves. One urgency is replaced with another. She would have to ignore it, this feeling, she thought. Or tonight her greatest danger would come from herself. Please hurry, she prayed silently. And don't let me want him like this.

As if in answer to her prayer, Aimeric spurred his horse past a tattered beggarwoman with a squalling infant in her arms and started up the ramp to the gatehouse of the Pont d'Avignon. He had to release her to pay their toll, and she drew the hood of her cloak securely over her head.

Aimeric took the bridge at a decorous trot, not wishing any

more than she to call attention to themselves. Leah could only stare with a mixture of fascination and shock. She had always thought of herself as somewhat world-wise. But she was little prepared for the sight of the night creatures who haunted the Pont d'Avignon.

There was the usual assortment of beggars and cutpurses, of course. She had expected that. No doubt a sinister figure or two could be found hugging the shadows of St.-Bénézet's Chapel. But most of the people on the bridge were women. They stood in pools of torchlight, calling out to prospective customers in raucous voices, some of their invitations sharp and clever, others slurred by drink. Their clothing was colorful, if not always clean, and their loose, disheveled hair fell unleashed about their shoulders. Here and there a breast popped gaily from the confines of a bodice, or a skirt was tucked up to reveal a fleshy leg. There were many soldiers and guards among them. But they were not patrolling to keep the peace; they were there to sample the wares.

The noise was cacophonous. The conditions were miserable. But the participants, for the most part, seemed to be good-natured. Where Leah had expected secrecy and stealth, there was instead a lively boulevard as public as the marketplace.

"Are you rich, handsome?" A plump red-headed tart grasped the bridle of Aimeric's horse, her hips swaying as she walked next to them.

"Not anymore," Aimeric answered, grinning. "My lady here has soaked me for every cent!"

At the sight of Leah swathed in her dark cloak and glowering even more darkly, the woman wandered away, winking broadly at Aimeric and giving the mare a slap on the rump.

Aimeric seemed quite at home on the bridge, Leah thought glumly. How easily he had spoken to that woman.

"Don't let them upset you." He spoke close to her ear. "We are almost through this part. They only gather at either end."

Aimeric spurred the mare onward. For a short distance beyond the torchlight, couples grappled in the shadows, moans peppered the thin moonlight, men and women laughed and argued, coins changed hands. Soon they rode into the long stretch of darkness that spanned the Rhône, toward the lights that beckoned from the cardinals' mansions in Villeneuve.

They had indeed passed through a secret world, thought

Leah, but one in which the mysteries belonged as much to women as they did to men. Did they feel powerful? she wondered. Or were they afraid?

Leah was only vaguely aware that she had been insulated by her father's wealth, protected by the tenets of her faith, by her sheltering community. For too long she had regarded these things as restrictive. So it was that she also failed to see a group of women enslaved by an irreversible poverty. Leah saw only their apparent range of choices, and a freedom that was unavailable to respectable women.

Riding through the darkness with Aimeric, she felt wild, separate from any world she had ever known and very far from home. There was nothing but the rhythmic movement, the odor of the horse, the river, the leather reins, the riders. There was the relentless heat, strangely thrilling.

The ladies at the Villeneuve end of the bridge were of a more exotic mold. They posed together in suggestive tableaux, their perfume wafting like clouds of mist on the cool night air. They were elegantly dressed in low-cut gowns, in fur-trimmed hoods, in veils that promised untold beauties beneath, in jewels, in single pendant pearls suspended like milky droplets between inviting cleavages. There were several boys among them, their loose shirts open to reveal doeskin chests; and an African in a brocade robe languishing at roadside as though he lay on the thickest of carpets.

In contrast to the aggressive hawkers at the Avignon end of the bridge, these haunters of the night were suggestively silent, as though their very existence was inducement enough.

"They are expensive amusements," said Aimeric, "for that cardinal or bishop who might be struck with a flight of fancy on his way homeward. That one, for instance, the golden-haired angel in the gown of yellow velvet, is a boy no older than yourself, famed for his beauty."

Leah's mouth dropped. "You mean he *chooses* to be a woman?"

"Are you so unhappy with what you are?" asked Aimeric gently. He spurred the mare and cantered up a winding ridge into the hills of Villeneuve.

Leah's heart was in her throat. It was time for the night's work to begin. So soon.

● ● ●

The mansion of Cardinal Bertrand Signac was situated on a rocky cliffside overlooking the Rhône. It was hidden from the road by a high stone wall, and bounded by forest on either side. The torchlit gate was guarded by two men-at-arms who chatted in the bored tones of watchmen who have nothing to watch.

Aimeric harnessed his mare to a tree well off the road on the near side of the property and walked with Leah into the dark wood. Together they emerged at the edge of the forest and studied the house in the moonlight.

The mansion was built of thick blocks of stone, buttressed at the sides and roofed with tiles. The lower floors were served by plain, rectangular mullioned windows, but the facade was embellished on the third and highest floor with narrow trefoil windows topped by crosses, in the ornate style of the Palace of the Popes. The entrance, a great pointed arch, opened onto an inner courtyard. It was protected by a portcullis, tonight half open like the mouth of a waiting mastiff.

"That's a good sign," Aimeric whispered. "It's likely the cardinal hasn't returned yet from the palace. But I see no way for you to get in. You can't just walk across the courtyard and through the door."

Leah was ready to strike out on her own. "Wait with your mare," she said. "If you hear any commotion, go back to the bridge. And if I fail to meet you there, return to Avignon. And Aimeric—I thank you."

"Good luck, then, Leah." Aimeric hesitated. Then, thinking the better of whatever gesture he may have been about to make, he disappeared back into the forest.

Leah shouldered the sacks of meat that Aimeric had handed her. "The dogs will be at the back of the house, near the stables," he had told her. "If you don't go near them, you may not even need this." But his words had given her an idea. There were other features at the back of the house. There would be the cliff, leading down to the river. Surely, somewhere near the sheer drop to the water, there would be a latrine. And it would most likely be in sight of a rear entrance to the household. Once inside, she would search for more of the wax needed.

Leah crept silently through tangled foliage. The latrine was simple to find. The odor emanating from the crude stone hut was distinctive, and recent deposits were strung behind it like a slimy tail just visible in the moonlight where a drainage pipe emptied onto the rocky cliff below. Inside, the hut was probably nothing more than a board with a hole in it. Even in rich men's houses, people still got splinters in their behinds. Leah had watched her father remove many a one. The servants got them, anyway, she amended. Probably the cardinal had his own polished privy somewhere indoors that would be emptied by a servant into the same accommodating Rhône.

As Leah expected, the hut was located on a direct line from the kitchen entrance at the back of the house, where the great chimney was still smoking and a single torch burned at the wooden door.

Leah waited patiently, breathing through her mouth, and was soon rewarded. A kitchen maid, her hair pulled back under a crisp white cloth, came out to use the latrine. The girl lifted the torch from its bracket and hurried through the kitchen garden as though her need was urgent. As soon as the girl was settled in the stone hut, Leah leapt through the darkness and slipped through the kitchen door.

She was in a gray stone vestibule with a small domed ceiling. Three wooden doors framed in pointed stone arches opened ahead of her and to either side.

"Is that you, Marie? Back so soon? Did you bring the herbs I asked for?" The shrill voice must belong to the cook, Leah thought. It was coming from the door to the left, from the side of the house where she'd seen the great chimney. Leah tiptoed to the door ahead of her. It creaked as she pushed it open.

It opened onto a dining hall. The room was long and narrow, and the walls were hung with tapestries that fell almost to the floor. The floor was tiled with multicolored squares, in softly glazed designs of birds and florets arranged in a pattern as artful as an oriental carpet. A huge table, draped in white cloth embroidered at the edges, and benches of polished oak ran the full length of the room. Against one wall, a sideboard was heaped with treasures to rival the Pope's: etched silver platters and knives with jeweled handles, mazers of silver, ewers of crystal, goblets of gold. At the head of the table, a carved high-backed armchair, canopied in red, awaited the master of the house. Before his place at table stood a miniature silver ship, a jeweled *nef* castled fore and aft, bearing a cargo of salt and spices.

Near a second door at the front of the house, a low fire flickered in a stone hearth. Oil lamps cast a warm glow on the sideboard. But the *nef* gleamed in a brighter light. Next to the cardinal's place at the head of the table, in an elaborate golden candelabrum with three curving arms, burned three fruity-smelling candles of rich maroon wax.

Eureka! Leah licked her thumb and forefinger and extinguished the candles, each with a satisfying hiss. Pulling them from the little spikes that held them in place, she stuffed them down the front of her dress and headed for the wooden door that would take her back to the vestibule and then to the kitchen garden. But someone was coming!

The door flew open and the cook strode into the dining hall, her hands on her broad hips. She wore the habit of a Benedictine nun, but both her demeanor and her speech had more in common with an overworked countryman's wife.

"Marie, where are you, you lazy girl?" she demanded. Leah cowered behind the door, willing herself invisible.

"Just look at this table! I thought I told that strumpet to fix new candles in here. She's left bits of wax from the old ones about, like a rat leaves crumbs. Useless girl!"

The woman bustled out, leaving the door wide open. Leah did not move. Soon the cook returned with a fistful of candles, which she lit at the hearth and jammed onto the candelabrum one by one. "Hmmph!" was her remark. She returned to the kitchen, pulling the door to the dining hall shut behind her.

All was quiet. Leah crept from her hiding place, her heart pounding, and opened the door a crack. The cook was bustling noisily in the kitchen. Leah slipped into the vestibule, toward the garden door. But again someone was coming. Marie!

The third door in the vestibule was her only choice. Leah ducked inside. She found herself in a huge pantry, dimly lit by a single small lamp.

The wooden shelves on the stone walls were stocked with dried foods of every kind. There was a great barrel of salt and jars of grains, kegs of flour and crates of dried fruits and nuts. In one corner there were spices, in another soaps and oils, and in a third . . . Leah almost groaned aloud at the irony. There were dozens of candles, all made of fruity-smelling maroon wax.

Hiding two more of the candles in her bodice with the others, she lifted the oil lamp from its hook in the wall and listened for sounds from the kitchen. Then, shielding the lamplight with her cloak, Leah slipped back into the kitchen garden.

That was easier than it might have been, she thought, breathing a sigh of relief. But how was she to find a patch of monkshood in the dark, in a garden as large as the square outside the synagogue?

Suddenly the vestibule door swung open again and a grumbling Marie emerged, grabbing the torch. "And don't you forget the savory, neither," the shrill voice followed her into the night. "It's in the section next to the sage!"

Leah threw herself flat on the ground beside a row of overgrown squash. The vegetables would have been harvested some weeks before, but Leah was grateful for the generous ground cover the huge leaves still provided. Marie was at the other end of the garden, tsking and whining to herself. "Call me a useless cow, will she? And me suffering from the bellyache! What am I to do? I bring her the marjoram, I bring her the basil, and now she wants savory. And soon we'll be bringing them all in to dry, she says. I never could tell a sprig of parsley from a thistle bush! Which one is this, then?"

Leah breathed slowly, the candles pressing into her chest. She'd been a fool again, she realized. The cardinal would never grow monkshood in his own garden, where it would more than likely wind up in his own dinner! But with the understanding came disappointment. She would have to return to search the woods by daylight. Where else would one cultivate a poisonous plant? They would have to delay their plans—for a sample of aconite was a crucial ingredient in the plot she had cooked up with Scorpio and Zarah.

Marie took her doubtful finds back into the kitchen, and Leah began the precarious journey back to the forest. She didn't want to cross the garden, in case Marie reappeared. It would be best to cross the darkest expanse of yard to the latrine again, then skirt the cliffside until she reached the forest.

Halfway across the yard the barking began. Two enormous mastiffs bounded around the corner of the house. Trailing their leather leads loosely behind them, they made a beeline for Leah. The moonlit dogs, huge black snarling shapes in spiked collars, their teeth dripping wetly like bloodied daggers, looked like they could tear a horse in two. They must smell the meat on her! Dropping her lamp with a strangled cry, flinging the sacks of meat into the garden, Leah raced for the latrine and slammed the door, the slavering beasts close on her heels.

"Herod! Samson!" The voices of two men-at-arms followed on the heels of the dogs. "They've trapped someone in the latrine again," said one. "Probably Marie," guffawed the other. "She's been in and out of here all day! Ho, Marie, is that you?"

"Who else would it be?" called Leah in a whiny voice. "Get them beasts out of here, or I'm never coming out!"

The mastiffs barked wildly, sniffing the ground outside the latrine, jumping up against the stone hut, snorting and growling.

"You dropped your lamp, Marie," the first soldier called. "It's still lit, though. I'll put it on the ground outside, you can pick it up when you're done."

"Thank you—oooh, what gas!" Leah groaned, and made a rude noise.

"Let's get out of here," said the second soldier, holding his nose.

"Aye, before Sister Stewpot comes scolding at us for chasing one of her girls. Herod, down! Samson!"

Grabbing the protesting dogs by their collars, regaining control of their leather leads, the men-at-arms hauled them away.

When all had fallen silent, Leah found she was trembling. She could have been mauled to death, or perhaps worse, captured as an intruder. What could she have been thinking of, coming here like this? Peeking from the latrine, she was strangely touched by the pale light glowing from the little oil lamp the kenneler had placed against the side of the hut. And then she fell to her knees in the damp mud and wept with joy. The dog's claws had raked the earth at the foundation of the hut, tearing loose the clumps of plants that grew there. Uprooted and mud-spattered, cast against the latrine wall and outlined in the light of the lamp, was a stalk of monkshood.

Aconite. The spindly plant was growing on both sides of the

latrine. The heavy purple flowers, climbing the stalk like a clothes tree hung with cowls, were just finishing for the season. It made perfect sense, Leah thought, almost amused. What better place than a latrine to grow the deadliest of blooms? No other place could afford such a constant stream of high-quality manure, yet be so rigorously avoided by anyone who had no need to be there. Surely no one lingered here to admire the flowers!

Leah gathered several plants, then sped into the forest to search for Aimeric. It hardly mattered to her to find that he wasn't there, and the mare was gone. Wearily, she began the walk in the dark down the hillsides of Villeneuve-lès-Avignon toward the Bridge of St.-Bénézet.

"Psst! Leah, is that you?" She had only gone several yards when she heard the familiar voice and a faint whinny. He was waiting for her, after all. "I heard the dogs and thought I'd better move to a safer place. Are you all right?"

Leah nodded, allowing herself to be lifted into the saddle and delivered to the bridge. It was very late. The colorful denizens of the night had long since dispersed. She was suddenly so very tired. Aimeric's arms around her felt safe and good.

"You were very brave to do what you did," Aimeric was saying.

"Hmm?" She must have fallen asleep. She and Aimeric were at the center of the Pont d'Avignon.

"But we'd best get rid of this." Aimeric took the little oil lamp that had been swinging gently at the mare's side and flung it into the night. They watched it until it was swallowed by the silent river somewhere far below.

The darkness was complete. They were utterly alone. Leah felt the creeping warmth again. Aimeric was holding her very close.

"Did you find what you were looking for?" he murmured, pressing her to his chest. Leah nodded dumbly, her mind whirling. His breath was on her face, his lips were on her cheek, at her neck. She had told him she would do anything to thank him—maybe it wouldn't be so bad. The heat was swelling in her belly like a wave.

"What's this?" Aimeric sounded annoyed. The hard wax

candles in her bodice were digging into his ribs.

Leah withdrew one of the candles. "It's to make a doll," she said.

"A w-wax doll? Like the one in de Gascon's bed?"

"This one's for Signac," said Leah dreamily, pulling him back to her. "I needed special wax."

Leah felt Aimeric stiffen and then thrust her away, as if with an effort of will.

So he is a virtuous man, after all, thought Leah, making no protest. It was for the best. It was just the night, the fear, the proximity of a handsome savior. She might have succumbed. But Aimeric had behaved well.

They rode back to Avignon in silence, Leah satisfied and relieved, Aimeric almost frozen with terror. So she was a sorceress! Soon she would practice her fiendish art on Bertrand Signac. And he was all alone with her in the night! She must have put him under her spell, he could see that now. It's a good thing he hadn't coupled with her, or he'd be in her power forever.

Chapter
16

*O*n the night of the following day, Scorpio waited patiently in his place of concealment behind a floor-length tapestry in the darkest corner of Cardinal Bertrand Signac's dining hall. He was sorry that Leah could not be here to watch what was to come. But it wouldn't have been done for the cardinal to think the de Bernays were in any way involved.

Like most of the high-ranking courtiers in Avignon that night, Cardinal Signac was dining on fish, a gift from Pope Clement's own kitchen. He signaled for his favorite servitor, a long-lashed boy of almost indecent beauty, to deliver his covered dishes from the sideboard and to pour him a goblet of wine. But the cardinal preferred to dine with no distractions, and the boy soon withdrew.

The soup was fine and the fish was delicious. The cook had outdone herself tonight, he thought. What could this be? Chewing greedily, he pulled the next dish toward his place. He lifted the ornate domed cover from the silver trencher, smacking his lips in anticipation.

Scorpio watched triumphantly as the cardinal grabbed at his throat and made a choking noise. As the cardinal began to splutter, unable to speak to call for his men, Scorpio swallowed his own mirth and practiced a fierce expression.

The cardinal's face had purpled in horror. Silhouetted on the platter, artfully arranged on a bed of aconite leaves, was the chubby figure of a red wax doll in a little wax cardinal's hat, holding a sprig of still-flowering monkshood, fashioned with loving glee by Grandmére Zarah.

Scorpio stepped quietly from his hiding place and into the candlelight at Signac's elbow. The cardinal, who had been unable to take his eyes from the offending dish, looked up at the appearance of the rustling red gown.

"*Aiieeeeh*!" The screech of terror would surely be heard throughout the household. Soon the men-at-arms would come running. The cardinal fell to quivering, whining in Latin in a sniveling voice, making the sign of the cross in Scorpio's direction. Scorpio knew what Signac must see: a fearsome devil of the brightest red. For, attired in the round, flat hat and scarlet robe that had once belonged to Arnaud de Gascon, his skin had changed to match.

Scorpio stepped forward and spoke to the cardinal in his watery voice. "Tell your household not to be alarmed. Send your men away. *Now*!"

Scorpio withdrew into the shadows as clomping footsteps resounded from the front of the house. An armed guard pounded at the wooden door and marched into the dining hall.

"E-everything is fine," croaked the cardinal. "I-I thought I saw a rat. Wait outside until I finish my meal."

The guard turned sharply on his heel and left the room as a nervous servant peeked through the door at the kitchen end of the house. Before he could speak, he, too, was waved away.

"So, Bertrand Signac, do you see this?" Scorpio emerged from the shadows, brandishing a stalk of the poisonous monkshood plant. "I do hope you have enjoyed your delicious dinner. I learned the recipe from you—the very recipe you so thoughtfully passed on to Arnaud de Gascon just before he, er, came my way."

The cardinal clutched at his throat and gagged. "Devil! Begone!" Staggering backward from his thronelike chair, he thrust a finger deep into his mouth and tried to eject his dinner.

"I see you are familiar with this plant," Scorpio continued smoothly. "But look closely. Do you not recognize me? I can cure you of the effects of this poison, just as I did for Arnaud de Gascon. Don't you remember?"

Signac froze and peered closely at Scorpio.

"I only ask a simple favor of you," said Scorpio. "Unless, of course, you prefer to die in agony, as did your victim, whose death throes you yourself witnessed in their entirety.''

Signac fell to his knees and moaned, as though he could see Arnaud de Gascon before him, screaming in pain, writhing in delirium and finally rattling in a burst of terror as his spirit escaped him.

''I see you remember,'' said Scorpio. ''You would do well to hurry, for you have but two or three hours before the poison takes you. You'll know the sequence when it starts, of course. The tingling sensation all over your body, the feeling that your hands are covered with fur.'' He paused. ''Then the chills and shivering, as though you had snow in your veins instead of blood. There is the agonizing pain, naturally. Inability to move or escape. The madness, the yellowing of your vision that leads to blindness. And finally, sweet death, delivering you to my care forever.''

Scorpio was quite enjoying his acting job. He wished the de Bernays could have witnessed the fruits of their scheme. The cardinal was in tears on the floor.

''Heal me, Satan,'' he pleaded. ''What would you have me do? I will do it.''

Scorpio drew himself to an imperious height and held the sprig of aconite over the cringing cardinal. ''Call for your finest horses and carriage. Your time runs short. Together we will visit Pope Clement VI.'' Signac looked up at Scorpio beseechingly, whimpering and nodding obsequiously. ''You will confess to the Pope the murder you have committed for which an innocent man has been doomed,'' Scorpio commanded. ''If you do this, you will live.''

Chapter
17

"*P*ssst! Your Holiness!"

The Pope groaned.

"Forgive me, Your Worship, for rousing you at this late hour, but it is a matter of the utmost urgency."

Scorpio watched with satisfaction from a shadowed corner of the papal bedchamber as Bertrand Signac, now close to panic, struggled to awaken Pope Clement VI. From his great bed the Pope, swathed in white linen, drew a coverlet of fur over his head and snored, flopping onto his stomach like an Arctic seal.

"Your Holiness, *please*!" Signac grasped the holy shoulders and shook.

The Pope rolled onto his back and pulled himself up into his pile of bolsters and cushions, grumbling and rubbing his eyes. He seemed taken aback to see Signac; as his mouth opened in a surprised "O," an extended, almost melodic burp emerged, and with it the faintest odor of the evening's wine.

"Bertrand, what in blazes are you doing in my bedroom in the middle of the night?" The Pope hauled himself fully upright and pursed his lips. Cradled in a sea of covers in his close-fitting white nightcap and gown, his features pink and puffy with sleep, Pope Clement VI was hardly the authoritative imperator Scorpio had expected. At this moment he resembled more a royal piglet, irrationally swaddled and all too vulnerable. Could this be the man whose wisdom and might could unravel the mysteries of the orb?

"Forgive me, Most Holy Father," Signac entreated, falling

to his knees at the edge of the bed and kissing Clement's doughy hand. "I have been visited by a devil, and I must do as he says, or I shall die."

Clement's aspect changed, and Scorpio decided his first impression may have been hasty. Fully awakened, the Pope was commanding and assured.

"So they're back, are they?" he demanded, throwing his covers aside and displacing Signac in the bargain. "Hand me my robe, I shall be but a moment." Accepting the ermine robe that Signac proffered from the end of the bed, Clement disappeared into his study.

Signac paced nervously, wringing his hands and wiping the sweat from his brow. He looked terrible, haggard and unshaven, his usually elegant features collapsed, his pallor deathlike.

"Already I am chilled to the bone," he whined, addressing the shadows where Scorpio stood motionless. "I will tell him as soon as he returns, you can be assured. I beg you, remove this curse from me!"

"Until you confess your crime, you are doomed," Scorpio replied evenly.

Signac crossed from the bed to the hearth, where he warmed himself at the low fire, then back to the bed again.

"Bertrand, are these the devils who visited you?" The Pope returned from his study with a small painting. "Did they carry with them a glowing ball?"

"Only one visited me," Signac stammered. "And he is—"

Scorpio shook his head and Signac caught the cue.

"—and he has poisoned me, *just as I poisoned Arnaud de Gascon*! There, I've said it. Forgive me, Your Holiness, but I must speak quickly, or I shall die as well, poisoned by the devil who haunts me."

"Then speak, by all means!" Clement waved a hand in alarm.

"He has bade me to make a full confession to you."

The Pope looked confused, but agreeable. "Very well, Bertrand, if it will ease your soul. I will hear your confession. Shall we adjourn to the chapel?"

"If you please, I must do this now, without delay."

The Pope signaled that the cardinal should continue. Signac's words came in a rush.

"Forgive me, Most Holy Father, for I have sinned. I took the life of my brother Arnaud de Gascon while in the pay of the Viper of Milan."

Pope Clement VI looked angry and weary. Signac took a breath.

"As *you know*," he continued pointedly, "Arnaud de Gascon was critical, even rancorous on the subject of the Archbishop of Milan. He had gone so far—too far, many thought—as to recommend that Giovanni Visconti be excommunicated." Signac paused. The suggestion was not without reason, he knew. It was said that the Archbishop of Milan had only celebrated Mass once in his entire life, and on that occasion he had dropped the Host! But the power and riches of Giovanni Visconti could not be ignored, even if he was a poor sort of churchman. It was the survival of the Church as an institution that mattered, was it not?

"Visconti controls Bologna now," Signac continued, his words tumbling forth as he raced to excuse himself, even as he hastened to save his own life. "Without the Milanese, we will lose all control in the Papal States. The Holy See is already living on loans, there is the Crusade to worry about, and this endless war between the English and the French, not to mention the expenses of the court . . ."

Clement waved his hand impatiently. He had to listen to enough of this sort of talk from the *camerarius*, without hearing it from a confessing cardinal.

". . . in short, without the revenues of the Visconti, our own treasuries will be exhausted. Information came to me that de Gascon was in the pay of the Florentines, the enemies of the Milanese, that he was spying on their behalf . . ."

Signac's words trailed off. He mopped his brow.

"And since you are in the pay of the Visconti, the unpleasant necessity of removing de Gascon fell to you?" prompted the Pope.

Signac hung his head.

"Are you not aware that I have entered into negotiations with the Visconti?" demanded Clement. "It was unnecessary, this murder! The Florentines have made their objections well known to me. But last year, when we needed their help to combat the Visconti in Bologna, they refused. They thought they could triumph over the papacy and the Milanese both. Now they fear that the Visconti will devastate Tuscany! Arnaud de Gascon was a foolish man. But *you*, Bertrand—you have been more foolish still!''

The Pope sighed, then focused his attention on Signac again, as though he had suddenly remembered that he was hearing a confession, not leading a political discussion. ''And you have committed a grave sin.''

Clement and the cardinal prayed in Latin, and the Pope gave Signac his blessing. ''We will speak again to determine your penance,'' said Clement. ''But there is more I would know. This devil you speak of—there was just one?''

''Only one, Your Worship. His coloring was red, but his face differed from the devils in your painting. And he carried no such ball of light.''

''You must have seen the third demon, the one whom I seek,'' the Pope said smoothly. ''If you see him again, tell him I would speak with him.''

Signac clutched at his throat and looked anxiously into the shadows.

''As I would speak with you, Your Holiness,'' said Scorpio, stepping forth. The startled Pope made a sign of the cross in the air before him, but quickly regained his composure. Scorpio made similar motions as he circled the pathetic figure of Bertrand Signac, who was complaining of the pains in his chest. What a weakling this murderer is, he thought, and what a powerful force is a guilty mind. He and Leah hadn't poisoned him, of course. But Signac looked as though he might obligingly curl up and die if left to his own imagination.

''Aconite, begone,'' Scorpio pronounced. With a grateful little yelp, Signac grasped the hem of Scorpio's robe and made as if to kiss his feet. Scorpio wrenched his robe from the cardinal's hand and stepped backward. ''The curse is lifted. You will live.'' He waved Signac away. The cardinal breathed a great sigh of relief and stood erect, his features regaining a measure of rather sullen dignity.

''We will meet again by day,'' Clement said graciously. ''You are no doubt in need of rest. And Signac—I am obliged to you for delivering this, er, gentleman to my presence.''

Signac nodded and fairly flew from the chamber. At last

Scorpio would have his audience with the Pope.

"You must be Scorpio," the Pope began, turning to fetch the painting he had commissioned. "I have met two of your friends. Do you recognize them?"

Clement VI studied Scorpio as Scorpio admired the painting of the Hunters. This devil was shorter and slighter than the other two, and different about the face somehow. Less predatory. But he was costumed in cardinal's red, the same color as his skin, and Clement took the message as a powerful *memento mori*—even the officers of the Church could be condemned, he was reminded. But Clement had made his own confession, and his conscience was clear. His gluttony was well under control—he wasn't that fond of fish—and he hadn't been with a woman since the other two had visited. There was certainly no sin in trying to win the Orb of the Pantocrator for the Holy See.

"They want your ball of light, your orb," Clement added.

"So that is why you have set your men on me. They have threatened you unless I deliver the orb?"

Clement VI declined to respond.

"These others are evil," said Scorpio. "But I seek knowledge of this orb. It is said that you have such knowledge."

So, the orb did exist! Clement's eyes glinted greedily. What a coup it would be to own such a treasure! And then he would vanquish all three of these damned devils—it couldn't be too difficult, judging from the reports his men had brought him from the marketplace.

"Bring the orb to me," Clement commanded regally. "Then you shall see what I know."

"I will bring it to you tomorrow," said Scorpio. He was beginning to worry that if he stayed in one place much longer, the Hunters would locate him. It was time to finish his business and flee back into hiding. "I will bring you the orb after you free Nathan de Bernay, the Jewish doctor who was falsely accused of the murder of Cardinal de Gascon. I will bring his daughter to witness your act."

Scorpio was pleased. He had kept his part of the agreement with Leah, and Nathan would be freed. It appeared the Pope had some knowledge of the orb and its workings. Perhaps he would soon be on his way back to Terrapin.

• • •

Pope Clement VI was less than pleased. He had sympathy for the Jew, but he could hardly accuse one of his own cardinals of murder. The scandal would be enormous, and his court was riddled with scandal enough. The Jew was convenient.

Why should the devil care for the Jew, anyway? Unless he was a Jewish devil—could that explain why the other two were pitted against him? Could that be why Scorpio didn't seem to know how his own orb worked?

Clement's mind was racing. It could be that he was witnessing clear evidence of a new spiritual truth: As above, so below. As on earth, so in Hell. Perhaps even in the underworld, the souls of the Jews battled with the souls of the Christians. Of course, it was hardly likely that a Jewish devil would appeal to the Pope. Then again, Clement was known for having protected the Jews during the Black Death, provided them a haven from persecution in Avignon.

And what of the orb? Clement had stared at the painting of the Hunters for hours, ignoring the devils and trying to recapture in his memory the hypnotic intensity of the beautiful, swirling light. How could such beauty reside in the underworld? It was a thing of Light.

Clement VI was stumped. No matter how he posited the relationship, he couldn't decide how Scorpio and the Jews and the other two devils were connected. But he was certain of one thing. The two devils would be returning for Scorpio, and he would be pleased to deliver him. But first, before they showed up, he would take possession of the Sacred Orb. It belonged with the Vicar of Christ on Earth: the Pope. Its place was in the Light.

Chapter
18

*L*eah couldn't remember when she had been happier, or more nervous. She had barely slept, or been able to sit still, since Scorpio reported the news of Signac's confession. Today her father was to be freed, and at last she would have her day at court. Afterward, there was to be a celebration at the synagogue. All of the Jews of the quarter had turned out to wish her well, for they felt that the cardinal's confession had vindicated not only Nathan de Bernay but all of them.

Leah was wearing her best clothes for the occasion; everyone had agreed that she couldn't have looked more beautiful. Her gown was the color of sunlit amber, and was trimmed in sapphire brocade. Suspended from an embroidered headdress that was dotted with tiny pearls, a delicate veil fluttered lightly about her face, and settled like a cobweb on her long black hair. Her mantle was velvet of a rich forest green, bordered with marten's fur of golden brown.

Beneath the cloak, Leah was perspiring. She and Scorpio were to be received at court by Pope Clement VI himself.

As she followed Scorpio through the broad arched gate of the Papal Palace, Leah held her breath in anticipation of her first sight of the Palace Square. She breathed outward in awe. The crenellated walls, turrets and towers were positioned just as she had expected them to be. But even though she had watched the newly finished wing being built, even as she had seen the walls rise to fill the sky above Avignon, still she had not imagined the overwhelming power of the space the walls must contain.

An elegant squire, one of the hundred or so attendant to the Pope, hurried forward to meet them. Bowing courteously to Scorpio and Leah, but unable to hide a flash of curiosity, as though they were honored ambassadors from an exotic land, he indicated they should wait and disappeared through a gaping arch in the massive wall to the right. Above the arch, overlooking the courtyard from its lofty second story, was the Pope's Indulgence Window, a lacy rosette supported on spindly columns through which the faithful could be blessed.

Leah's awe was tinged with satisfaction. The palace was even more glorious than she had imagined. It positively soared. Of course, this was not the way she had imagined she would see the Papal Palace—accompanied by a demonic Benedictine at whom everyone stared openly with thinly disguised fear. Leah was not unaware of the steady, surreptitious trickle of chamberlains and chaplains, couriers and curates who seemed to have arranged that their duties would take them through the corner of the Palace Square where she and Scorpio waited.

Leah watched as Scorpio, once again pale beneath his Benedictine habit, adjusted his cowl to cover his face. She was as happy for him as she was for herself. He would accompany her to the Audience Hall, and would stay to secure the release of her father. Then, together, he and the Pope would examine the orb, and if all went well he would find a way to return whence he came.

Leah smiled. Scorpio had been so kind to Grandmère Zarah this morning, regaling her with the tale of Signac's fright, praising her waxen handiwork, teasing her gently for worrying, reassuring her that Nathan would be at home in time for the Sabbath. "The cardinal found your culinary masterpiece irresistible," Scorpio had told Zarah. "Never have you prepared a finer meal! That grinning—or should I say grimacing—little doll was the perfect main course. And the garnish! Flowering monkshood, rather than parsley—a most creative touch!" It had been good to hear her grandmother laugh again.

How terribly she would miss him, Leah suddenly realized. For all the fury he could evoke in her, and for all of the miseries for which she couldn't help but blame him, he had taught her much, and been a better friend than any other she had known.

The squire returned. "I am to escort you to the Hall of Great Audience," he announced. "You are to have a private audience with the Pope." He inclined his head respectfully toward the deeply shadowed arch. "Few are so honored."

Leah resisted the urge to take Scorpio's hand as they were ushered across a dimly lit passage. Master porters stood aside to let them pass at the entrance to the Hall of Great Audience. They descended a flight of stone steps. Each step was circular, each wider than the next, so that they seemed to spread into the chamber below like a wave. Leah felt dizzy, and vaguely diminished, as though she had shrunk to the height—and been beset by the fears—of a four-year-old.

The Great Audience Hall looked to Leah like a forest of stone, vast, yet oddly intimate. Although it ran the entire length of the new wing, the space was divided into a series of bays, each with its own recessed window, and the whole was supported by a line of scalloped columns, their ribs splayed like the branches of thick, sturdy trees to form the peaks and arches of the ceiling. The ceiling itself was relatively low, its sections jointed like the wings of bats, as though a man-made cavern had been chiseled into a mountain of rock, with one side opened to the light of day.

At the far end of the hall, enclosed behind a circular barrier of masonry and regally enthroned upon a carpeted dais, Pope Clement VI awaited their progress. The Pontiff was resplendent in embroidered cloth of gold that hung from his shoulders in stiff, pyramidal folds, and he wore a miter that echoed the shape of the arches behind him, as if man and building were one. He was flanked by a sparse semicircle of various retainers, none of whom Leah recognized. A few of them appeared to be barristers, and several wore cardinal's red. Signac was not present; and the room was guarded by a ring of sergeants-at-arms. But for the most part, the wheellike arrangement of benches that were normally filled by the tribunal body known as the Rota were empty.

Leah and Scorpio approached the judge's dais and Scorpio pulled the cowl from his face. But if Clement was disconcerted by Scorpio's change, both of complexion and habit, from cardinal's red to gardener's beige, his expression showed only a slight, possibly even amused, lift of an eyebrow.

We must look as insignificant as insects to him, Leah

thought, squaring her shoulders and tilting her chin proudly upward to face him. But before she could speak, the Pope raised a single pink hand. He had spared her embarrassment, Leah realized. It would not have done for her to speak first.

"Allow me to confirm what your companion"—the Pope nodded to Scorpio—"has undoubtedly told you. I have heard the confession of a murderer, a personage of noble birth, who, by virtue of the sanctity of the confessional, I will not name. But be assured that the murder of Arnaud de Gascon weighs heavily upon his soul. No doubt the injustice of a false accusation weighs similarly upon your father, child. I will see to it that he is freed at once."

Leah turned to Scorpio with tears of gratitude in her eyes.

"And now, sir," continued the Pope, "I believe we have an urgent matter to discuss. Perhaps the lady will await you outside?"

Leah, elated, curtsied deeply to the Pope and whispered her heartfelt thanks. She wanted nothing more than to rush to the prison, to embrace her father as he walked through the gate. But she couldn't bring herself to leave without saying goodbye to Scorpio. She walked the length of the Great Hall of Audience as if on a cloud, admiring the painted frescoes and the carvings of fabulous beasts that crouched beneath each cluster of springing ribs. What a magnificent room it was! How could she have found it intimidating? By the time she reached the circular steps, Scorpio was hurrying to join her.

"I have told the Pope that the orb is on his own land." Scorpio's flutey voice held an edge of excitement Leah had never heard before. "He is eager that I should fetch it at once, and return with it to this chamber." He paused, as though he had been selfish in thinking of his own triumph first. Then, pressing Leah's hands between his own, he looked into her eyes. "Thank you for your help," he said. "I don't believe the Pope will go back on his word. Your father will be freed."

Scorpio's hands were warm and firm, like the hands of any man. And he had thanked her, when she felt nothing but gratitude toward him. Leah felt a pang of loneliness, as though Scorpio had already gone. She searched for a way to tell him goodbye. "Shall I come with you to fetch the orb?" she asked, suddenly shy. She pulled her hands away, hoping for a reprieve.

• • •

Clement VI waited until he was certain the smug little devil, the leper-healer, the demon sorcerer, or whatever he was, was out of earshot. "Follow him, and bring me the orb," he ordered the captain of his private guard. "When you have it, you can kill him, but be neat about it. All of Avignon will want to see the body of this devil laid out in the Palace Square. And you may as well pick up the girl while you're at it. She's obviously learned her sorcery from her father."

"I would like you to come with me," Scorpio replied simply. He turned and walked up the rounded steps. Behind him, two flickering lights gradually grew brighter.

"Scorpio! The Hunters!" Leah screamed in horror and raced past Scorpio for the archway, pulling him into the passage that opened to the Great Courtyard beyond.

The lights seemed to leap in the air, and the Hunters materialized in the center of the Palace Square, blocking the exit to Avignon. There they stood, their crimson faces grim and determined, their arms crossed fiercely over their chests, their black robes settling around their ankles as though the cloth had been lifted by some spirit wind.

"This way!" Scorpio clutched Leah's hand and dragged her back into the passageway. "Run!"

A long, narrow corridor spanned the outer length of the Audience Hall. A short distance along the corridor, a stairway led upward.

Tiny beams of light, like the reflections of pins, flashed against the stone wall behind Leah's head, leaving crumbling hollows in the block. Leah and Scorpio flew up the spiraling staircase to emerge on the floor above the courtyard. One wall danced with the afternoon shadows of the pierced rosettes in the Pope's Indulgence Window. Opposite the window was yet another arch, a magnificent arch with a monolithic lintel, carved on the left with angels leading souls to Heaven and on the right with the damned in the fires of Hell. A pier at the center of the arch held a statue of Saint Peter, who separated a pair of gargantuan wooden doors.

Scorpio pulled Leah through one of the doors, the door on the angels' side. It closed with a resounding roar.

"Oh, God," Leah cried weakly. They were in a chapel, a

space more vast than the Cathedral of Notre-Dame-des-Doms, as long as the Audience Hall and three times as high, an airy space filled with miraculous sunlight. Their footsteps echoed to the Gothic heights as though they were dancing across a skin drum. On the walls were tapestries, none of which reached to the floor, and a simple stone altar faced rows of wooden pews, carved and low. There was no place in which to hide.

"This door," insisted Scorpio, pulling Leah onward. A small tierce-point door opposite the altar led to a sacristy. "You must get away, or they will kill you. They only want the orb."

"No, they want *you*—they also want *you*!"

The Hunters burst into the chapel as the sacristy door swung closed. From the sacristy, a very long, narrow corridor, unlit and windowless, led to the private apartments of the Pope. Scorpio pushed Leah ahead of him. She felt herself running, running. In the distance, as if through thick stone, she thought she could hear the barking of dogs.

The corridor hooked sharply to the right and Scorpio and Leah emerged in the Pope's private dining room. Two doors opened on the far side of the room. Scorpio looked through one, and exclaimed with recognition.

"This is the robing room! I passed through here with Signac last night. The Pope's bedchamber is just beyond it. You must hide in there. You'll be safe. I'll take the other doorway. I think I can find my way out of here. Adieu, Leah!"

Leah turned desperately to Scorpio. How could she leave him like this? They would kill him! She could hear the Hunters in the narrow corridor. Soon they would both be caught.

"Go! There is no time!"

Leah turned toward the robing room as Scorpio had ordered.

"There they are! After them!" A contingent of the Pope's men-at-arms appeared in the robing room. "You're ordered to kill the leper on sight!" barked one. "And beware of the devils he commands. But take the girl prisoner!"

Again, Scorpio pulled Leah into a narrow passageway to safety. "Betrayed!" he whispered bitterly, running, running.

"Wait!" hissed Lethor, freezing at the entrance to Clement's dining room. "The Pope's men will capture them for us!"

Waiting for the guards to thunder through the chamber, the Hunter commander beckoned to Ardon the Stalker to follow.

The maze of corridors ended abruptly. There were no doors, no windows, only a stone wall leading to nowhere.

Leah clutched Scorpio, shielding him with her body. Six of the Pope's men-at-arms advanced on them. The men took their time, swaggering as they walked, their weapons drawn, but casually lowered.

"His Holiness Clement VI had several dead-end corridors constructed to foil would-be assassins," leered the captain of the guard. "Luckily for us, you've found one of them. Saves the breath."

Leah's eyes widened in terror. Behind the Pope's guards, the Hunters were silently advancing. They smiled grotesquely with each unhurried step they took, their faces a patchwork of raw, peeling flesh and sutured scars, souvenirs of their skirmish in the marketplace. Ignoring the guards, they looked only at Scorpio.

"Take us to the orb!" commanded the thin one, his words spitting forth in a snakelike hiss.

The Pope's men whirled on the Hunters, uttering cries of alarm. The devils were back, this time in the Pope's own palace! The captain charged, brandishing a sword at the heftier of the two, the one Scorpio knew to be Ardon.

In seconds, the captain of the guard was felled, a tiny hole smoldering in his metal breastplate. *Flash! Flash! Flash!* The devil had hardly seemed to lift a finger. Three more of the soldiers died instantly in brilliant bursts of light. Like magic, slender trickles of blood pooled at a throat, a forehead, in an eye socket. The final two soldiers collapsed to their knees, crossing themselves and praying.

Leah squeezed her eyes tightly shut, waiting for a piercing pain, for death to overtake her. Her head was filled with a rush of noise, as though her blood was gathering behind her ears. All at once she knew the sound: it was the barking of a pack of dogs, and the clamorous footfall of armed men.

Pope Clement VI, tall, lordly and angry, strode into the corridor and faced the scene. He was surrounded by a phalanx of guards, a many-layered human shield. The men in the foremost ranks could barely restrain their yapping dogs. The second rank held buckets of water at the ready. It was obvious that the Pope had been well briefed as to the scene in the market-place.

Clement VI drew himself up to his most regal height.

"The Orb of the Pantocrator is the rightful property of the Holy See," he intoned. "Devils, I banish you from my sight!"

Ardon and Lethor backed toward Scorpio and Leah until they stood possessively, one on either side of their quarry. Leah held her breath and Scorpio quivered as Ardon extended the daggerlike spikes at his wrist and pointed at the Pope.

"Loose the dogs!" commanded Clement.

"There is no more time for this nonsense!" hissed Lethor. Whisking an orb from beneath his robe, he and Ardon quickly encircled Scorpio and Leah.

Leah stared at the small, glowing, radiating haven of light.

Raising the orb above their heads, Lethor arched his fingers and pressed gently, as Ardon laced his fingers through Lethor's own.

In a blinding flash of sweet golden light, all four were gone.

Leah felt a feverish wave of heat engulf her, and a heady calm, as though she was stilled amidst turbulent motion. Was she in darkness or light?

Opening her eyes, Leah was petrified with disbelief. She and Scorpio were alone with the Hunters on the Rocher des Doms, the rocky cliff beyond the cathedral, near the gardens and the stables of the Papal Palace. How could they have gotten here? *The Hunters' orb*. In the distance, through her terror, she could hear the commotion of a gathering army, and the maddened frenzy of a pack of hunting dogs.

Ardon the Stalker held Leah from behind, his bloodred arm stretched across her throat like a slashing promise.

"Now, Scorpio," said the thin Hunter. "You know Ardon will kill you when he is ready. But I, Lethor, Assassin of the First Rank, tire of this planet and its inhabitants. I am prepared to spare the life of your little friend if you will lead us to the orb with no further resistance."

Guards and dogs were pouring from the palace. Ardon tight-ened his grip around Leah's neck and extended the stiletto lasers at his wrists.

"I will take you there." Scorpio met Leah's eyes, his look expressing the hope and the sorrow of frank defeat. Then he broke into a run.

Through flower gardens and vegetable patches, orchards and wooded trails, past the stables and the henyards, Scorpio ran with but one thought in his mind. *Reach the orb!* As he ran, his strength seemed to grow. There were wings sprouting from his ankles; he could almost feel them beating against the lovely humid air of this green planet.

Behind him, the Hunters followed briskly, their skins enflamed from their exertions in the moist atmosphere. Leah was with them; he could hear her light breath mingled with the Hunters' huffing. Not far behind them came the army of the Pope on the heels of their own stalkers, the highly trained dogs whose flaring nostrils, exquisitely sensitive, picked out the odors of the black-robed devils and hounded them hungrily.

Scorpio ran to the far end of the fishpond and stopped. Close behind him, the Hunters reached the pond and looked at one another in dismay. The pond was overflowing with shiny silver fish. Thousands of fish. They jumped from the pool like excited molecules and disappeared again below its surface. The water churned.

Ardon and Lethor fell to their knees, searching the pool for a glimpse of the orb, calculating whether a dousing of this magnitude would kill them, wondering to which of them the task should fall. At any moment the dogs would reach them. They must decide.

Leah stood at Ardon's side, momentarily forgotten. The fish flapped and splashed at the surface of the pool, their scales glittering in the sunlight. A clattering contingent of the Pope's men-at-arms charged into the clearing and made to loose their arrows at the Hunters. Light glinted from their armor, flashed from their swords.

In the split second before the lasers fired, in the briefest of moments before swordplay echoed through the papal clearing, Leah's eyes met Scorpio's. The look they exchanged was silent, mutual and instantaneous. With no hesitation, with the grace of diving birds, they plunged through the crowded, silver-packed waters to the bottom of the pond.

Chapter
19

"*S*wim, Leah, there is no turning back. Swim, now, like an Aquay!"

"Scorpio, I can hear you, I am swimming toward the orb. *The orb.*"

Their minds locked together in silent calm, Scorpio and Leah dove toward the vibrant light that glowed from the depths of the papal fishpond. Their arms, like wings, propelled them downward through a tangle of fins and gills. Schools of fish parted before them to open a path, then closed again to fill the gaps. Above them in the world of air, the water frothed with laserfire gone astray, with spears and arrows released by frantic crossbowmen, with wounded soldiers twitching at poolside, to die among asphyxiated fish.

Leah expelled the last of her air in a tiny stream of bubbles. Her black hair drifted around her in an inky cloud. She and Scorpio briefly watched the bubbles float upward. Above them, in a distant world, a battle was raging. Here and there a fish would explode like a silver wine vessel split at the seams, spilling its crimson innards in a burst of slick streamers. *Like comets*, thought Leah. *Like rockets*, thought Scorpio. The surface of the pond darkened with blood.

At the bottom of the pool, the water was stained a delicate pink. It filtered downward in rosy striations, illuminated like watered silk by the light of the orb. Scorpio and Leah reached forth as one. The orb seemed small, as though all but its core had dissolved, leaving just a ring of filmy light where once had

155

been solid matter. But as their hands passed through the honey-colored corona, as their fingers interlaced and arched against the orb's leathery surface, as they felt the pulsing leap of energy travel upward through their limbs, there was no denying its life-giving power.

Is this what death is like? wondered Leah. Is there a future, where time stands still.

Leah opened her eyes. They were still at the bottom of the pool. Seconds must have elapsed, but nothing had happened. She felt as though her lungs were about to burst.

Leah pushed upward toward the surface of the pool. The water was clear, and there were few fish. Next to her, Scorpio, too, was rising. Her eyes were closed and his cowl spread peacefully about him like the gown of an angel. Leah could just see that he held the orb close to his body, tucked under one arm.

Gasping for air, Leah dragged herself from the pool and rolled onto her back on the ground. Her clothing clung to her like a liquid stone, and her muscles ached with tension. But the air felt balmy and sweet.

Scorpio's head bobbed to the surface and he floated serenely for some moments. Then he swam, one-armed, to the edge of the pond as a fish darted merrily in and out of his wide, Benedictine sleeve. He seemed to be as at home in the water as the fish, Leah observed. She looked about the clearing in confusion. They were quite alone at the pond. The Hunters were gone, as were the Pope's men-at-arms. There were no barking dogs or clanking swords. Even most of the fish had disappeared.

"Are you all right?" Scorpio clambered from the water. "I thank the Deity you are safe."

"What has happened?" Leah examined their surroundings with mounting anxiety. "Everyone is gone. But we are still here, at the pond. I thought your orb would take us to a different place, just as the Hunters' orb somehow moved us from within the palace to without."

"I don't know," said Scorpio, studying the clearing. Something did seem different. The smell of the air. Or the trees, perhaps. He concealed the orb beneath his habit. How good it felt, the warmth, the weight. If only he could keep it with him always. He was pleased that Leah was unharmed. Perhaps her presence had somehow tied them to this planet. But no doubt Ardon and Lethor would come for them again. It was time to see her safely home, and then—on to Terrapin.

"I must go to my father," said Leah. "I must know that he is safe."

"But the Pope has ordered your arrest as well as mine." Scorpio lowered his voice, searching the trees for guards. "He betrayed us both, do you not remember?"

Leah hung her head. "Our plan has failed." Idly she began to wring the water from her dripping skirts.

"After dark, I will see you back to the quarter," said Scorpio. "Then we will find out what we may. You may have to hide, as I did, in the synagogue. Or even leave Avignon for a while. But I shall trouble you no further. The orb will take me where it takes me."

Leah nodded. She felt drained and defeated. Scorpio was right.

"We'd better conceal ourselves until we dry," she said. Her voice was flat. "There is a rocky ledge behind that stand of trees. We can sit there and catch the wind from the river."

Scorpio watched sadly as Leah disappeared into the trees. They *had* failed, and he might have gotten her killed besides. He should never have become so involved with the beings on this planet. And Leah's questions were bothering him. Why *hadn't* they been transported out of Avignon? Where had all the soldiers gone? And why were there *buds* on the trees?

Scorpio! Leah let out a terrified shriek.

Scorpio left the fishpond and hurried to Leah's side. She was sitting on a ledge of rock on a steep bluff. The view stretched beyond the Bridge of St.-Bénézet, across the sparkling Rhône to the hills of Villeneuve-lès-Avignon.

"What is it? What's wrong?"

"The walls—look! Avignon is surrounded by ramparts, *huge* stone walls, with turrets and gates—it couldn't be! They were not there this morning. It takes years to fortify a city so!" Leah turned to her companion, terror-stricken and trembling. "Oh, Scorpio, what is happening? Do you see them too? Am I mad?"

For Scorpio, what had begun as a faint suspicion was now confirmed. "It was the orb," he answered softly. "We *have* traveled, Leah. But we have not traveled in space—we have traveled in time!"

Leah's eyes widened, and she shook her head vigorously. "That is not possible. This cannot be happening. It is a dream." Suddenly she grabbed Scorpio's shoulders and shook him as hard as she was able. "Take me back! What have you done? *Take me back!*"

Scorpio was as stunned as Leah. He did not doubt that time travel was possible. But he felt more lost than ever, and overwhelmed by questions. How far forward had they come? If the orb allowed one to travel in time as well as in space, had he traveled in time when he left his own planet? What year was it now on Terrapin? Was he perhaps in earth's future, but Terrapin's past? Or vice versa? The questions wouldn't stop. How did the orbs work, what were their limits, had the Hunters mastered all of their powers, how had they used them to enslave his own people? Was he lost in time?

Leah stopped shaking Scorpio when he let out a prolonged, pained wail. But she remained seated with an arm about his shoulders. That he was as frightened and confused as she, she could see. Strangely, Scorpio's pain was almost a comfort to her. She was reminded again, and at last began to believe, that he was neither angel nor demon, but a being perhaps as unfathomable as her present situation was inconceivable.

Leah made an effort to face what she could see. Scorpio held back no secrets. He was lost. Therefore, they must unravel the mysteries of the light-filled ball; and she was as likely as he to find a way to do so. It seemed that fate, for whatever reason, had thrown them together, so together they would seek the answers they needed. If this was the future, so be it.

Leah's terror was gradually giving way to a curious excitement. None of the other girls in the quarter had had such adventures, of that she was certain.

"Let's do what we are able, one task at a time," she said to Scorpio. "Are you dry? No? Then let's stand on the ledge and study this new city." Helping Scorpio to his feet, Leah held her skirts and her hair to the wind. It must be early spring, by the feel of it, she thought, with just a hint of sun-warmed air blowing up from the river. It's afternoon, judging from the sun. She turned her back to the wind and looked toward the Palace of the Popes.

"Clement must have died," she remarked. "There is a new pope. Do you not see the arms on the banner that flies from the highest turret?"

Scorpio looked admiringly at Leah. Her approach to life was practical, he thought. The unanswerable she simply put aside, and her acceptance of the evidence before her allowed her great flexibility. If only the Aquay had been so clear-eyed! He watched as Leah scrutinized the view. Her curiosity and thirst for learning seemed to mitigate her fear of the unknown, though there was no doubting her courage. She had recognized his despair and had been sympathetic. She made no recriminations, and was patiently waiting for him to recover. To his surprise, Scorpio realized that he was describing a good friend.

"You have been very kind," said Scorpio. "Thank you."

"I am sorry to have shaken you. I was frightened. But now you have your orb back, and we have learned one way to make it work! You'll soon find your way to Terrapin." Leah's face was once again bright with hope. "I must look for my father. Perhaps things will be different now if Clement is truly dead. I say we should venture into town and find out what year it is. We can pretend to be travelers from a distant land."

As perhaps we are, thought Scorpio grimly. But he agreed. If they hadn't come too far in time, Leah could return to her home and he would be on his way. He would miss her.

Leah braided her hair and smoothed the folds of her skirt, brushed the velvet of her cloak and pressed the brocade edges of her sleeves. The soaking in the fishpond had done her finery little good, but she was presentable. Scorpio, his habit still damp and smelling like a wet sheep, looked as shabby as ever. That was perfect. He would be taken for a country priest come to seek benefices in Avignon.

Together, the unlikely pair descended from the Rocher des Doms.

"Excuse me, sir." Leah stopped an elderly gentleman just outside the cathedral, while Scorpio pretended to rest nearby. "I wonder if you could tell me how long the city walls have been here. I lived in Avignon as a child and have recently returned, but I don't remember them."

"You're quite right, girl," replied the man. "We've only had the ramparts, let's see, five years now. They were started in 1357, after the truce."

Leah did a quick calculation in her head, then glanced furtively, panicked, at Scorpio. It was 1361. They had jumped ten years. But the old man was looking at her strangely. She must conceal her shock. "T-truce?" she managed.

"The truce of Bordeaux, girl, between England and France. Put all of those Free Companies of mercenaries out of work, and now they're ransacking all of France. Isn't that why you're here? Taking refuge from the pillage? The villains!" The old man shook his head. "I see you've got all your finery on your back—you're lucky you got through at all. No wonder you're a bit addled. Why, the White Company is camped just south of here. If Innocent VI doesn't pay their ransom . . ."

The old man broke off. "There, now, girl, don't look so alarmed. There are patrols of the Pope's men everywhere, and more wooden barricades going up. You can hear the noise all over the city. You'll be safe enough in Avignon."

"I hope so, sir!" Leah answered. "But it's not the glamorous place it was in Clement's day, is it?"

"No, indeed!" The old man's eyes twinkled. "Those were the days—music, banquets, artists, ladies. Now, Innocent—he'd like nothing better than to finish his days in the monastery he built across the river, the Chartreuse. He'll get there soon enough, too, he's as old as me!" The old man cackled mischievously. "But Clement ran his court like a king! Cost him, too. . . ."

Leah left the old man to his ruminating and rejoined Scorpio. "It's been ten years," she said. "Shall I say I've been in hiding? In prison? How have I survived? How is it I haven't aged? Scorpio, how can I go home?"

All the while she was questioning, Leah was walking resolutely toward the Jewish quarter. She paused at the gate. That, at least, had not changed. Her face registered joy, and terror, nostalgia and resignation, all in a matter of seconds. At last she turned to Scorpio and embraced him briefly, ignoring the astonished stares of passersby.

"Scorpio, will you wait for me? I fear what I will find inside, but I must go by myself. Please, if I am not back in an hour or two, I hope you will find your way to what you are looking for.''

Leah slipped through the gate in the rue Jacob and disappeared into the winding alleys of the quarter. They seemed as crowded as ever, dark and smelly. She avoided the square and the synagogue, and entered the back garden of her father's house. A lamp was lighted inside, and the smoke from a cooking fire rose into the dusky sky.

Leah was not certain why, but she felt compelled to knock. Footsteps hastened to the back door.

The door was opened by a woman in her mid-twenties. Leah recognized her only with difficulty. She was Félicie Morel—a grown woman. She held an infant on one shoulder, and a small child clung to her skirts. At the sight of Leah she blanched as though she was seeing a ghost. Leah understood.

"Please forgive me for arriving unannounced," she began, "but I am a relative of the de Bernay family, seeking news of my relations. I was told they lived here?"

"Forgive me! Come in." Félicie introduced herself as Leah sat on a wooden bench near the fire. The kitchen looked almost the same. But new benches had been placed around the table, which was covered with a fine linen cloth, and a curtain of a crisp green fabric covered the tiny window that overlooked the garden.

"It's j-just that you look so much like one of the de Bernays. Her name was Leah. . . .''

"She would be my cousin, I believe," Leah said. "My mother and her mother were sisters.''

"I had no idea Madame de Bernay had a sister," replied Félicie. "She's been dead these many years.''

"What happened to the rest of the family? My cousin?''

Félicie looked stricken. "It is a tragic story," she began. "And you have traveled such a long way. Perhaps you would like to see the rabbi?''

"I am staying with my husband's family," Leah said. "We are only passing through on our way to Carpentras. But please, if you could tell me. . . .''

"They are all gone now, I am afraid," said Félicie. "The doctor, Nathan de Bernay, was executed ten years ago for the murder of a cardinal under Pope Clement VI." She paused as Leah turned pale. "Don't be ashamed. We all knew he was innocent. It is said that another cardinal was the true murderer. But of course, the Pope would never have allowed such a scandal to become public, not when there was a scapegoat handy. The Jews were bitter, and there were protests, of course. But the Church prevailed.''

Leah choked back angry tears. ''And my cousin?''

''Leah.'' Félicie shook her head in wonder. ''Her death is surrounded in mystery. The way the story goes, she was drowned with a mysterious stranger on the grounds of the Papal Palace. Her body was never recovered. Some say she was a sorceress, and that devils took her! Others say she was eaten alive, that Pope Clement kept sharks in his pond. You can see where she drowned still. There's a fishpond in the Pope's gardens. In Avignon, some people say they've seen her, and the stranger too, a monk, floating at the bottom of the pool, just faint, like shadows. People tell such stories! Am I frightening you?''

''No, please go on,'' Leah urged.

''Well of course, some say that Leah ran off with this monk, who was a leper, to live in a leper colony! She wanted to be a doctor, like her father, you see. And others say she didn't run off with a monk at all, but with a handsome young Christian knight!''

''A knight?''

''A nobleman's son. He went off years ago to join the Crusade. He used to court all of the Jewish girls back then.''

''How do you know of all this? Did you know her?''

''A bit. She was a little older than me. She was standoffish, and had too much book-learning for her own good. But she loved her father, that's what my husband says. He knew her. He says she was slaughtered by the Pope's men-at-arms, and that it was as simple as that.'' Félicie shrugged. ''My husband was a widower and a friend of the family's. He moved into this house to look after Nathan de Bernay's mother, Zarah. She would have been your grandmother too, I guess. What a pity you lost touch with the family! After the son and the granddaughter died, there was no one left, you see. Zarah was old and blind. She's gone too, about six years now. She was grateful for the help and the company, and spoiled my husband's older boy! She deeded the house to my husband.''

Félicie's voice grew brighter. "You must meet him. Will you stay for supper? Mossé will be home soon."

Leah's heart was breaking. She no longer had a home. Her family was gone, she had failed to save her father, and now she must leave the quarter, quickly and forever, for if Mossé recognized her he would be terrified.

Should she go upstairs for her clothes? But of course they would all be gone. Would they still have her father's herb chest? But there was no way she could carry it. Leah wrenched herself from the fireside and clasped Félicie's hand.

"Thank you for your time," she said warmly. "I wish you and your family all happiness. But I am afraid I must be on my way."

"I wish you a good journey, then," said Félicie. "You'd best hurry, for the gates close at sundown. It is a shame my husband couldn't have met you—you look so much like her."

Leah smiled and took her leave. Félicie's voice held a trace of honest regret. But her expression was one of unconcealed relief.

Once outside the quarter, Leah allowed herself to cry. Her grief came in waves, as the understanding of all she had lost became more and more real.

In a dark alley, on a filthy side street near the Pont d'Avignon, Scorpio held her by the shoulders and murmured words of comfort when he could. Toward morning, the orb grew warm at his belly and he pressed it gently against Leah's back.

Gradually, as dawn broke, Leah's sobs subsided. "If you'll have me, I'd like to come with you," she said to Scorpio. "We are both lost now, it seems." She began to walk.

Scorpio walked next to Leah in companionable silence. She seemed calm enough this morning. But she would have more grieving to do, he was certain, and drastic adjustments to make as well. He hoped they would soon find a place she could safely settle. Now, with the orb tucked warmly against his midsection, he felt the urgent call of Terrapin. He could never bring her with him. Or could he?

"You don't know how to work the orb well enough to predict

where we'll land,'' Leah said gently, as though she had read his thoughts.

Scorpio the Aquay turned to face the human creature, Leah de Bernay. Their eyes, separately, told stories of mingled despair and hope. Their eyes, locked together, found a mutual reserve of joy. This world they were in, this place in time, they rejected. Together they would reach for the future.

"Where shall we jump from?"
"How about the bridge?"

With the night sky still an inky indigo at their backs, Scorpio and Leah walked east across St.-Bénézet's Bridge, into the pink-washed dawn.